Amanda forced herself to look John squarely in the eyes. "I'm sorry."

"About Dad? You said that already."

"No." Completely unprepared for such a personal exchange, she groped for the right words. "We were best friends, and I never even called you after I left. I never meant to hurt you. I just needed more than I could find in Harland."

"Y'know, for a long time I prayed you'd decide you made a mistake and come back." His expression closed up, his eyes darkening with a nasty mix of anger and pain. "You never did."

Over the years she'd convinced herself that he must have forgotten her and gone on to marry someone who adored him shamelessly. But he was her age—thirty-one—and there was no ring on his left hand.

"I'm here now."

"Because you've got nowhere else to go. I actually think that's worse."

As he stalked away from her, she wished there was something she could do to make things right between them.

Books by Mia Ross

Love Inspired

Hometown Family
Circle of Family
A Gift of Family
A Place for Family

MIA ROSS

loves great stories. She enjoys reading about fascinating people, long-ago times and exotic places. But only for a little while, because her reality is pretty sweet. Married to her college sweetheart, she's the proud mom of two amazing kids, whose schedules keep her hopping. Busy as she is, she can't imagine trading her life for anyone else's—and she has a pretty good imagination. You can visit her online at www.miaross.com.

A Place for Family

Mia Ross

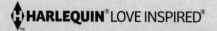

Recycling programs for this product may not exist in your area.

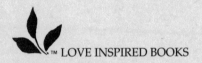 ™ LOVE INSPIRED BOOKS

ISBN-13: 978-0-373-81683-5

A PLACE FOR FAMILY

Copyright © 2013 by Andrea Chermak

www.LoveInspiredBooks.com

Printed in U.S.A.

Let us not love in word or talk
but in deed and in truth.
—*1 John* 3:18

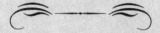

For Rob

Chapter One

Perfect. Just perfect.

Amanda Gardner pulled onto the side of the deserted country road as what she'd assumed was steam took on the alarming smell of smoke. To be on the safe side, she shut off the engine and popped the hood release. Not that she'd know what she was looking at, she thought as she left the disabled car. But maybe opening the hood would dispel some of the heat and the engine would start again in a little while.

Sure, she grumbled to herself as she looked through the crack for the rusty latch. *And pigs could fly like hummingbirds.*

When she touched the hood with her palm, she realized something was very wrong. It felt hot enough to cook eggs over easy, and she instinctively pulled away. Good thing, too. As she backpedaled on her Italian heels through the dusty gravel, the engine burst into flames.

A few months ago, she'd had a promising career in advertising and public relations, and a splashy condo in Malibu. Now, here she stood, completely incapable of doing anything but stare. She was vaguely aware of a strong arm pushing her aside and someone stepping in front of her with a large fire extinguisher. When she recovered enough to get a good look at the man who'd come to her rescue, she gasped in surprise.

John Sawyer.

The rangy farm boy who'd lived in her memories all these years had grown into an Adonis dressed in faded jeans. She thought he'd actually gotten taller, and the pale blue T-shirt he wore sculpted its way around muscles the guys she'd known in Los Angeles couldn't have built in a year at the gym. Those kinds of muscles you could only get working your entire life on a farm. And this guy had them to spare.

The girls had drooled over him during high school, and now he was absolutely irresistible. He must have to fend off every unattached woman within ten miles. Not that John would even think of refusing female attention, she amended with a little grin. If she remembered correctly, her childhood best friend had always taken all that very much in stride.

Once the flames died down, her rescuer flung open the hood and doused the engine with the last of the foam.

"Whew! That was close." As he looked at her, she saw no hint of recognition in his summer-blue eyes. "Are you all right, ma'am?"

"Ma'am?" she echoed with a laugh. "Are you serious? You've known me since we were four."

He studied her for a few seconds, then cocked his head like a confused hound. "Amanda?"

The humor of the situation dispelled some of the terror she'd felt watching the car she'd just been sitting in erupt in flames. "I know it's been a while, but I can't believe you didn't recognize me."

After assessing her from head to toe, he came back to her face with a disapproving frown. "You look a lot different than the last time I saw you."

Thirteen years ago, she recalled sadly. The day she hugged him goodbye and got on a plane, headed for UCLA.

"I guess so." Shoving the bittersweet memory aside, she asked, "How have you been?"

"Fine." He gave her wheels a skeptical look. "Where'd you get this heap?"

"From a girl in California," Amanda replied as vaguely as possible. Although she was looking directly at John, it was hard not to notice that he was focused on the car. She had a feeling he wasn't any more pleased about their unexpected reunion than she was.

"Hope you didn't pay her too much."

It had cost her a valuable vintage watch, but Amanda thought it was best to keep her dire financial straits to herself. For now, and maybe forever. She hadn't decided yet. "She gave me a good deal."

Obviously uncomfortable, he glanced around before meeting her eyes. "So, what brings you by?"

"I had an interview in Kenwood and was on my way back to that cute new B and B outside of Harland."

"It's been there ten years."

Amanda felt a flush creeping over her face, but she forced a smile. "It's new to me."

After an awkward silence, he asked, "How'd your interview go?"

"I was overqualified," she confessed with a sigh. "Just like yesterday and the day before."

John gave her a long, hard stare. She wasn't fishing for sympathy, but she didn't know what to make of his nonreaction. She'd known him most of her life, and she'd never seen him this closed-off. No, she corrected herself. She'd once known him very well, but she'd been gone a long time and hadn't gone out of her way to keep in touch. They might as well have been strangers.

To avoid his cool gaze, she glanced around at the fields surrounding them. The tractor he'd obviously driven up on sat across the road from her car. It was mid-May, and green shoots of various crops stretched out for what seemed like miles. The buzz of more tractors floated in on the warm breeze, and she took a deep breath of air scented with the first cutting of hay. Accustomed to the exciting, nonstop pace of L.A., she'd forgotten how it felt to stand somewhere and just breathe.

"The place looks great," she complimented him. "You must be really proud."

Folding his arms, he pinned her with a suspicious glare. She couldn't recall his ever being anything but wide open and friendly, and she had a feeling she was one of the few who'd ever seen that scowl on his sun-bronzed face.

"We're scraping by," he said curtly. "Some folks prefer hard work to glitz and glamour."

"I'm done with all that, and the advertising and PR agency, too. I'm coming home." Not completely by choice, but she had no intention of discussing that with him.

"Uh-huh."

"I don't care if you believe me or not. It's the truth."

"Whatever." When she glowered back at him, he shook his head in typical male bewilderment.

"You look a little flushed. We should get you in outta the heat."

The thoughtful suggestion soothed her frayed nerves, and she gave him a grateful smile. "Sounds good to me."

She opened the back door to get her one bag. A no-name duffel, it made her long for her matching set of Louis Vuittons. Then again, you didn't need Louis when you'd sold most of your clothes. At least she'd managed to keep the gorgeous Prada shoes she was wearing. Custom-made, they wouldn't have fit anyone else. Still, she'd worn them to the auction, just in case any of those bargain-hunting divas got any bright ideas.

After slamming the door closed, she realized that her bag smelled like smoke. That meant all the clothes inside did, too. Considering the endless string of horrible circumstances she was currently mired in, she should be glad they hadn't been reduced to ashes. Fortunately, her suit had escaped the worst of the smoke, which meant she could avoid the cost of dry-cleaning it. Although pickings were proving to be very slim, she was hoping she'd need it for more interviews.

John held out his hand, and she couldn't imagine what he wanted. "What?"

"I know you've been in the big city awhile," he answered with a crooked grin, "but around here, guys don't let ladies carry heavy bags."

"Oh." She blinked, then said, "It smells awful."

"That's okay," he replied as he swung it onto his shoulder. "So do I."

They both laughed, and John saw some of the tension leave her shoulders. As he started across the open field, she stopped him with a disgusted noise.

"You're kidding, right?" she demanded, as if he'd suggested they walk to the moon.

He pointed toward the house in the distance. "It's quicker to cross lots."

"Not in these." She angled her ridiculously high heels so he could see what she meant.

"So take 'em off."

"And drag these gorgeous Armani trousers through the mud? I don't think so."

"It's half a mile if we walk up the road." She gave him a chiding look, and he sighed. "Fine. Whatever."

John changed course and fell in step beside her. She seemed preoccupied, which gave him a chance to assess this near-stranger who had interrupted his plowing.

He didn't like what he saw.

As if the shoes weren't enough, her navy pantsuit was cut pretty close to the bone, giving her an angular, almost masculine appearance. Maybe it worked in L.A., but John didn't think much of it. For some crazy reason, she'd flattened her natural curls so she resembled a blond version of Cleopatra. Then there was the makeup. Applied with a trowel, it was photo-shoot perfect but covered the dusting of freckles that used to pop up on the bridge of her nose.

Even her personality seemed to have changed. He didn't remember her being so fussy, but spending years in a big, hectic city like Los Angeles would probably do that to anyone. Since he'd never lived anywhere but Harland, he wouldn't know.

When he realized they'd trudged along in silence for quite a while, he searched for something to say. "How're your parents liking Arizona?"

"Fine. Dad's dropped six strokes off his golf handicap. He says if he'd retired sooner, he'd be headed for the Champions Senior Golf Tour by now."

"And your mom?"

"Is the activities director at their condo's community center. She knows everyone and everything that's going on there, so she's happy."

Something in Amanda's tone seemed off to him, but they hadn't seen each other in so long, he couldn't be sure about it. And even if he was right, it was none of his business.

"Yeah, she always did throw a good party. Is your brother out there, too?"

"He and his family live in Wisconsin. How about the Sawyers?" she asked. "Are you all still around here?"

"Yup. You remember Caty McKenzie?" When she nodded, he went on. "Well, she married Matt, and they had Hailey a couple months ago. Marianne married his best man, Ridge Collins, last year, and now they're adding twins to the two kids she already had. And Lisa married Ruthy's nephew, Seth, last month. They're in Europe on their honeymoon right now."

"Wow! There's been a lot going on." After a few moments, she paused and pulled him to a stop. "I heard Ethan passed away a few years ago. I'm so sorry."

Coming out of the blue that way, her sympathy hit John like a truck. The latest in a long line of farmers, he wasn't the type to fret about things beyond his control. You worked hard and planned, then you adjusted when life threw you a curveball. There had been plenty of those in the last three years, starting with his father's wrenching death from a heart attack.

The tragedy had affected the Sawyers in some remarkable ways. Matt finally came home and mended fences with Marianne, then settled in Harland for good. It made Marianne rethink her priorities, and she was one class away from earning her master's in teaching. It even encouraged baby sister Lisa to use her artistic talent to start an interior-design business.

John hadn't changed, though. He was still trying to come to grips with the fact that if he'd been paying more attention during that long, hot day of haying, their father would still be alive. Matt and the girls kept telling him he couldn't have known anything was wrong, and he had to quit blaming himself. So far, he hadn't been able to manage that.

When he realized Amanda was watching him, he jerked himself back to the present. "Thanks."

"I know how much he meant to you. It must have been really hard."

Sympathy shone in her vivid blue eyes, coming through the phony makeup with an honesty that told him his childhood best friend was still in there somewhere.

Sure, he scoffed silently. The friend who had flown across the country the day after graduation and promptly forgotten all about him. No phone calls, no letters, no emails, nothing. It was as if she'd kicked the dust of Harland off her fancy shoes and never looked back.

Being a Sawyer boy, he'd appreciated girls for as long as he could remember. Tall, short, slender, curvy, blonde, brunette or redhead—it really didn't matter to him. He enjoyed them all, and they returned the favor. John wasn't in the market for anything serious, and he was always up-front about that.

Amanda Gardner had been different. His best friend, the one who always listened when he talked, even if he didn't say things quite right. The one he confided in when his latest girlfriend baffled him. He and Amanda had been close for so long, he'd thought she'd always be in his life somehow.

Until the day she wasn't.

He'd waited for her to contact him, give him an address to send letters to, something. Anything. As the years went by, he wondered about her less and less, until he finally decided she was gone for good. Of all the girls he'd known, it was the one he'd trusted most who had hurt him. Girlfriends came and went without causing all that much damage.

Losing his best friend had broken his heart. Since it looked as if she was actually moving back to Harland, he had to make sure that didn't happen again.

When John fell silent, Amanda felt horrible for upsetting him. Ethan's death seemed long ago to her, but obviously for John the pain was still very fresh. Expressing her condolences was appropriate, she reminded herself, the polite thing to do.

She hadn't meant to make him sad. Still, she felt awful about it.

Sensing that John was angry with her didn't help at all. Not that she could blame him for that, since it was her fault they'd grown apart. She wondered if everyone in Harland would give her the same kind of cool reception he had. With a mental sigh, she resolved to be patient and do her best to restore the connections she'd allowed to lapse. It had been easy to let them go when she'd been so far away. Now that she was back, rebuilding those neglected relationships could mean the difference between success and failure.

Finally, in the shade of an oak tree, Amanda saw the hand-carved sign that had stood in the same spot since long before either of them was born.

Sawyer Farm.

Those two simple words brought back a flood of wonderful memories, and they turned onto a dirt lane shaded by a canopy of ancient white oaks. Weathered split-rail fences bordered the winding driveway that led to a rambling white farmhouse. With broad, welcoming porches, it was framed by gardens filled with every kind of flower that grew in this part of North Carolina. Just walking toward that house made Amanda feel that things might actually work out for her.

Eventually.

They went up the back porch steps, and John dropped her smoky bag on the bench near the door. "That's seriously all your stuff?"

"Unfortunately, yes."

Questions sparked in his eyes, but to his credit he didn't voice any of them. "You used to take more than that to church camp."

It had been ages since she'd even thought about church, so John's mention of those simple, carefree times made her squirm. "I travel a little lighter now."

Without responding, he opened the screen door and motioned her ahead of him. Despite his chilly attitude toward her, the gentlemanly gesture was a nice change from fending for herself. She'd been struggling for months to pull her life together in L.A., as one friend after another abandoned her. While John hadn't exactly rolled out the red carpet, at least he hadn't turned away when she needed his help.

"The living room looks a little different," he warned in a hushed voice. "The doctor put Marianne on bed rest a couple weeks ago and she'll be that way till she has the twins."

"When are they due?"

"August tenth. Doctor says if she makes it to the end of July, he'll be happy."

John sounded nothing like the carefree farmboy Amanda remembered so fondly. The one who'd gallantly stepped up to be her date when her boyfriend broke up with her right before their senior prom. The one who'd paid the DJ to play a set of country ballads especially for her. Under the mirrored ball, with a corsage of tiny pink roses and baby's breath strapped to her wrist, she'd spent a blissful evening in John's arms. She'd been to the Academy Awards twice and countless Hollywood parties, but that dreamy high school dance was still the most perfect night of her life.

Looking at him now, she noticed some deep cracks among the laugh lines that bracketed his eyes. Worry, she realized. It didn't look good on him, but it told her that the generous heart he'd always worn on his sleeve was still alive and well. That was something, anyway.

A cute redhead materialized in the doorway, giving John a flirtatious smile. She was eyeing him as if he was her favorite dessert, and Amanda wasn't surprised when she batted her long eyelashes.

"Hey, handsome," she cooed. "I was hoping to run into you."

Clearly not put off by the very obvious display, he flashed her a grin that could weaken the knees of any female on the planet. "Hey yourself, Ginger. What are you doing here?"

"Interviewing for the nanny job. I think I'd be perfect for it, don't you?"

Her honey-pie drawl made Amanda want to gag, but John didn't seem to notice. After making a show of thinking it over, he nodded. "Could be."

The woman might be perfect for something, Amanda mused, but domestic goddess wasn't the first option that came to mind.

"Could you put in a good word for me?" Ginger asked. "This would be a great job for me, since I just love your niece and nephew."

Her supposed affection for the kids was such a thinly veiled act, Amanda couldn't help getting in on the fun. "Oh, that's nice. What are their names again?"

Ginger blinked at her as if she'd just noticed someone else standing in the kitchen. "Keith and Emma."

John's barely suppressed grin told her the nanny hopeful had missed the mark. Satisfied that she'd correctly nailed Ginger's intentions, Amanda called up a friendly smile. "I hope it goes well for you."

"Thanks!"

After another adoring look at John, the clue-less woman flounced down the steps and out to a sunny-yellow VW bug. It was the ideal car for John's not-so-secret admirer, Amanda thought. It wasn't like her to be so smug, but every once in a while she met someone so transparent, she just couldn't help it.

Grinning, John shook a finger at her. "That wasn't very nice."

"What are the kids' names?"

"Kyle and Emily. It still wasn't very nice."

Amanda recognized that he was trying to sound stern, but the twinkle in his eyes gave him away.

"She's an empty-headed moron obviously more interested in you than your sister's children. I can't imagine she'd have gotten the job even if I wasn't here to point that out." An idea popped up, and she sighed. "Is she your girlfriend?"

"Nope. Just a friend."

"One of many, no doubt."

Her harsh tone surprised her. Evidently, John was still the fun, great-looking guy he'd always been, and it only made sense that he'd have his pick of the women around Harland. Who he chose to date—or not date—was none of her business.

Her grumbly train of thought was interrupted by a question from the living room. "Is that Amanda Gardner I hear?"

The fact that Marianne recognized her voice after all these years gave Amanda a warm, fuzzy feeling. She took the cue to step into the doorway and wave. "Hi, Marianne."

She groaned. "Oh, don't stand out there in the kitchen. It's such a mess."

The sink was stacked with soaking pans and

dishes, and a jumble of boots and shoes were piled near the door. Some schoolbooks and a newspaper were strewn across the table, but it really wasn't all that bad, and she said so.

Marianne's laughter plainly said she disagreed. "You're so sweet. Come on in."

John moved aside and let Amanda go in first. A quick glance at him showed her no emotion on his face at all. She couldn't tell if he was upset about her calling Ginger out or couldn't possibly care less. The way things had been going for her lately, it was probably the second choice.

When Marianne saw her, she recoiled with the same shocked reaction John had. Quickly, the expression shifted to the kind a Southern lady plastered on when she disapproved of something but would never dream of saying so.

"Well, just look at you," Marianne gushed in a motherly tone. "You're so stylish, you could be on the cover of one of those Hollywood magazines."

She wasn't criticizing exactly, but she wasn't pleased, either. Trying not to take it personally, Amanda changed the focus from herself to Marianne. "That's nothing compared to what you've been up to. A new husband wasn't enough? You had to go for the jackpot with twins?"

"I know, it's crazy." Marianne nodded toward the man sitting in a wing chair beside the bed. "This is my husband, Ridge Collins."

Standing, he offered his hand. "It's great to meet you."

His clothes were covered in dust, and she asked, "Did Ginger interrupt your plowing?"

"Something like that. I don't think she's the right one for us," he added, giving John a very male grin.

"She's the fifth one we've interviewed, and none of them could find their way around a kitchen, much less keep up with the kids. The guys will only get busier over the summer, and I've got no idea what we're going to do," Marianne confided. "Things are getting out of hand around here, and we really need some help."

"I could do it." When they all stared at her, Amanda backtracked. "At least until you find somebody permanent."

Understandably, Marianne looked confused. "I thought you were in advertising and PR."

"The company I worked for went out of business, and the market out there is terrible, so I'm moving back here." Because she didn't want to get into the humiliating details, she decided to skip over the worst of her recent experience. "I'm not finding a lot of advertising or PR jobs here, either. This could be the solution to both our problems."

The Collinses traded a long, dubious look, and

Amanda held her breath. She could almost hear the wheels spinning in John's head, but he didn't say a word. Maybe he'd already guessed why she'd returned to Harland, or maybe he didn't care. Whatever the reason, she knew her respite wouldn't last.

If she was around the farm every day, eventually he'd ask her why she'd come limping home in a car that was one step from the crusher. But right now, she kept her attention on her prospective new boss, who was studying her pensively.

"Amanda," Marianne finally said. "Why on earth would someone with an MBA and a promising career in PR want to be a housekeeper?"

Several answers flashed into her head, all of them very grown-up and responsible sounding. But what came out was, "I'm ready for a fresh start, and Harland seems like the right place to do that. I've always loved this farm, and it would be great to work here."

John grunted. "Funny. After we graduated, you couldn't wait to get away from it."

Turning to him, she explained. Again. "I was eighteen and had never been farther than Charlotte. When UCLA offered me that scholarship, I decided it was time to get out into the world and see what I could do."

"And how's that working out for you?"

His accusing tone sliced through the air with a sharpness that stunned her. It was resentment, she realized with a sinking heart. Resentment she'd caused because in her driving compulsion to leave her roots behind, she'd hurt the sweetest, most solid guy she'd ever known.

"Not very well." Swallowing a bit of her pride, she included the others in her view. "I'm not exactly Mary Poppins, but I'm a quick learner. If you tell me what you want, I'll make sure things get done your way. I'll even work free for a week," she added to sweeten the deal. She'd picked up that skill during her stint in online PR, and she hoped it would help her now.

Marianne and Ridge exchanged another look, and she could only imagine what they were thinking: Why is she *really* here?

They didn't say it out loud, which Amanda really appreciated. As she'd told them, she just wanted a chance to start over. Once she had a steady paycheck, she'd answer all their questions. Even John's. His wariness toward her wouldn't make it easy to be around him all the time, but she'd have to cope as best she could. With her nicely toasted car still smoking out on the shoulder, she'd literally reached the end of her road.

The fact that her twisting path had led her back to the Sawyers didn't escape her. When she was younger, John's large, loving family had treated Amanda like an extra sibling. Now, Amanda needed Marianne as much as Marianne needed her. If not more.

"We can't pay much, so we were offering live-in arrangements," Marianne ventured. "Would you be staying here?"

"Ordinarily I'd say no, but since my car—"

"Broke down out front," John interjected smoothly. "She'll have to stay here awhile."

Amanda snuck a quick glance at him, but couldn't tell if he liked the idea of her being so close by or not. She didn't remember his being this difficult to read. Had he changed, or had she lost her touch? Either way, it was a complication she didn't need, and she resolved to get her own place as quickly as possible.

Cocking an elegant brow, the lady of the house flat-out asked, "John, would Amanda's working here be a problem for you?"

After enduring so much phoniness in California, Amanda found it refreshing to be around people who came right out and said what was on their minds.

To her relief, he shrugged. "I work all day, then go down to my place, so it wouldn't matter to me."

"I won't be doing much of anything for the next

three months," she reminded him. "That means Amanda would be running the house, including the kitchen. If you want to eat, you'd have to see her at some point."

"No problem here." He looked at Amanda. "You?"

"Not for me." Sensing she was on the verge of getting a "yes," she pressed. "I could start now, if you want. I'd be happy to do some laundry and cleaning before the kids get home from school."

"We haven't discussed your weekly salary." Ridge named an amount she'd have laughed at six months ago. "Does that work for you?"

"Definitely." It wasn't much, but it was significantly more than the $82 currently in her wallet. Besides, Harland was pretty far off the beaten path. Money would stretch a lot farther here than it had in L.A.

After another wordless conference with his wife, Ridge nodded his approval.

"We'll give it a try," Marianne announced with a smile.

Amanda wanted to hug her, but with Marianne laid up in bed, she knew that was a bad idea. Instead, she clasped her hands tightly and gave them her warmest smile. "Fabulous. Thank you."

She wanted to assure Marianne and Ridge they hadn't made a mistake, that she would do everything in her power not to let their family down.

But these were down-to-earth folks, and overblown promises meant nothing to them. She'd show them, though, and make the Collinses glad they'd taken a chance on her.

Chapter Two

Fabulous, John silently echoed Amanda.

That wasn't quite how he'd describe it, but for Marianne's sake he kept his opinion to himself. He had a hard time envisioning his old friend in this flashy woman standing in their living room, but she just might be the answer to their prayers. If she was as capable as she claimed to be, hiring her would keep the house running smoothly while the farm spun on its usual seasonal axis.

All his life, John had trusted in God's wisdom, even when it made absolutely no sense to him. If this was His solution to their problem, John would have to find a way to put aside his wounded pride and make it work.

Standing, Ridge bent down to kiss his wife's cheek. "Unless there's another interview, I should get back to cultivating that cornfield."

"We're done for today. I'm sorry we wasted so

much of your morning," she added with a scowl of disapproval.

He grinned. "It wasn't a waste. I got to hang out with you."

"Maybe tonight you can finish up early enough to have supper with the kids and me."

"I'll do my best." Lifting his hand in a general goodbye, he sauntered out the front door.

"You look tired," John told Marianne as gently as he could. "Get some rest, and I'll show Amanda where everything is."

"Thank you." Wincing, she placed a hand against her side and leaned back into her pillows. "I think they're kickboxing in there."

"You want anything while I'm around?" he asked.

"No, I'm fine."

"Just yell if you need me," Amanda piped up. "I won't be far."

With a wan smile, Marianne pointed to the cell phone docked on her night table. "Ridge texts me every ten minutes."

"That's so sweet! But you can tell him to stop worrying and keep both hands on the wheel. It's probably not safe to drive one of those big tractors while you're texting."

"That's what I told him, but my husband's a very stubborn man. He didn't listen."

"I'm here now, and I'll take care of everything. You can all relax."

Their unlikely nanny-slash-housekeeper glanced at John, and he responded with a "we'll see" kind of look. A lot of water had flowed under that bridge—some of it bad. Just because he was being nice didn't mean she was off the hook. She'd wanted different things than he did—that much he'd understood. Over the years, he'd quit waiting for her to write or call, recognizing that it meant she was happy in her new life. Forgiving her had been tough, but eventually he'd done it because it was the right thing to do.

Forgetting her had proven impossible.

He was trying to act cool, but he had to admit that knowing she'd driven across the country in that death trap of a car really worried him. If she hadn't jumped out when she did, she could have been killed. That stark realization brought all kinds of old feelings rushing back, and he was having a tough time getting them corralled again.

Her story about moving home seemed sincere, but he didn't quite buy it yet. She'd left Harland once, he reminded himself. If things didn't shake out the way she wanted, he wouldn't put it past her to do it again. He'd never been able to predict what was going on in that quick mind of hers, and his gut was telling him that hadn't changed. If he wanted to keep his sanity, he would be smart to keep a respectable distance from her.

Leading her back into the kitchen, he pointed to the side porch. "Laundry's out there." Then he nodded at a closed door. "Cleaning stuff's in the pantry, along with the food that's not in here, the fridge or the freezer downstairs. We've got a dishwasher now, and this is where everything goes."

He opened cupboard after cupboard, leaving them open for her to look inside. Then he pointed up. "The kids' bedrooms are obvious, Ridge and Marianne's is across the hall. The guest room is at the end of the hall."

"Got it."

"Bathroom upstairs, another one down here." A movement outside the window got his attention, and he grinned, grateful for the distraction. "Oh, and the kids' dog. You need to meet him with one of us or he'll go bonkers on you."

They stepped outside as a muddy black Lab was making a beeline for the unfamiliar car parked on the side of the road. He skidded to a stop when he heard John whistle, looking from him to the car as if trying to decide which was more interesting. In the end, he chose John and loped over to greet him.

John hooked the Lab's dusty stars-and-stripes bandanna in his fingers and reeled him in before he could jump on Amanda. "This is Tucker, the best dog in North Carolina."

"Hey there, Tucker." Kneeling down, she held out her hand for him to sniff. "Nice to meet you."

After a quick assessment, he apparently decided she was okay and flipped onto his back in an unmistakable plea. Laughing, she rubbed his belly, mud and all, while he licked her arm in appreciation.

"You always did have a way with guys," John said as he got to his feet.

"It's a gift."

"If you say so."

John tucked his thumbs in his back pockets in a gesture she remembered well. As he looked down at her, Amanda tried to gauge what he was thinking. John had always been wide open and genuine, with a quick smile and a laid-back demeanor. That charming country boy still lived in her memory, frozen in time the way he'd looked when she last saw him.

Over the years, she'd convinced herself that he must have forgotten her and gone on to marry someone who adored him shamelessly. But he was her age—thirty-one—and there was no ring on his left hand.

Standing, she forced herself to look him squarely in the eyes. "I'm sorry."

"About Dad? You said that already."

"No." Completely unprepared for such a personal exchange, she groped for the right words. After a mental shake, she jammed her brain in gear and continued. "We were best friends, and I never even called you after I left. I never meant to hurt you. I just needed more than I could find in Harland."

"Y'know, for a long time I prayed you'd decide you made a mistake and come back." His expression closed up, his eyes darkening with a nasty mix of anger and pain. "You never did."

"I'm here now."

"Because you've got nowhere else to go. I actually think that's worse."

As he stalked away from her, she wished there was something she could do to make things right between them. She wanted nothing more than to have her old buddy back, yanking on her braids and tossing her fully dressed into the pond while he laughed and dove in after her. John hadn't stood in the way of her getting this job she so desperately needed, but he hadn't completely accepted her, either. With a sigh, she realized that might be the best she could hope for.

Tucker pulled her out of her funk when he stood on his back legs and wrapped his filthy paws around her waist. Her designer trousers would need to be cleaned, but compared to what she'd been through lately, that was a minor inconvenience.

Laughing, she ruffled his fur. "At least you like me. What say we get you rinsed off and then do some laundry?"

Seeming to understand that she'd asked him a question, he barked and led her around the corner of the house to a coiled-up hose. He stood at attention, wagging his tail as if he couldn't wait for a good dousing.

"Tucker, you're amazing." He barked again, the corners of his mouth crinkling in what she'd describe as a canine smile. She pressed the trigger to start the water, and he clumsily lapped up several mouthfuls. When he'd had enough, she turned the hose on his fur. "I think you and I will get along just fine."

When he shook himself out, he drenched them both, making her laugh again. Realizing that she'd done that more today than she had in months, she smiled. Despite the trouble still nipping at her heels, it was good to be home.

What was Amanda doing here, anyway? John wondered as he climbed aboard his tractor and turned the key. Nothing. He gave it another shot with the same result. He should have known better than to shut it off, he grumbled to himself as he jumped off. The temperamental old engine would need a half hour before it was cool enough to restart.

Resigned to waiting, he slid down to sit in the shade the oversize back tire made on the ground.

"Problem?" his big brother, Matt, asked as he strolled over.

"Just the usual." Trying to look unconcerned, John crossed his legs at the ankles and got comfortable. "No big deal."

"That's not what I meant." Matt sat with his back against the other side of the tire and unscrewed the cap from a thermos of sweet tea. He swallowed some, then held it out for John. "I noticed we've got company. Pretty company."

After a swig, John answered, "Amanda Gardner's back."

"For how long?"

John shrugged. "Last I knew, she had a great job in L.A. and was all wrapped up in her fancy new life. Her parents moved to Arizona after her dad retired. If she needed a place to go, she should've gone there."

"Wonder why she didn't."

"Who knows why women do anything?"

Matt chuckled and nodded toward the blackened clunker sitting on the shoulder. "Advertising and PR folks usually make good money. Wonder why she's driving that pile of junk."

"She said her company went out of business, so she lost her job."

"Why didn't she get another one?"

Once John had filled him in on the details, Matt hummed. "A fresh start makes sense, I guess. But why come back here?"

"Like I said before," John snapped, "I've got no idea."

Angling his head, Matt grinned over at him. "You're wondering, though, aren't you? And it's making you cranky."

"I'm hot, not cranky." Hearing the sharpness in his tone, he tried to smooth out the edges a little. "Amanda does what she wants, no matter what anyone else thinks."

That should have aggravated him more now than ever, but for some crazy reason it didn't. It had always baffled him why he'd let her get by with so much attitude when he preferred girls who were sweet and uncomplicated.

Setting the thermos on the ground between them, John rested his head against the wheel and sighed. "I always liked that about her."

"Women like that are nothing but trouble."

"Oh, spare me," John scoffed. "You married a woman like that."

"Caty's different."

"'Cause she's the mother of that baby girl who's got you wrapped around her little finger."

"Partly." Smirking like a man hopelessly in love with his wife, Matt sipped some more tea. "You think there's more to all this than Amanda losing her job?"

"Probably. Can't imagine her driving all this way otherwise."

"What're you gonna do about it?"

Staring over the fields toward the house, John rolled the question around in his mind. She'd been his friend once—closer than any other he'd had—but over the years his opinion of her had taken a lot of turns, mostly for the worst. Seeing her again had shaken him, no doubt about that.

To combat those feelings, he just had to remember that she'd left him behind for something she wanted more. L.A. drew her in with the promise of excitement and money, both of which she'd probably had more of than he could begin to imagine. And when whatever had chased her off resolved itself, she'd return to her career because that was what mattered most to her.

"Nothing," he finally said. "It's not my problem."

Matt cocked his head in disbelief. "You don't mean that."

"Yeah, I do. Whatever mess she's in is her own making, and it's got nothing to do with me."

Getting to his feet, John hauled himself up to the tractor's seat and actually crossed his fingers.

When the engine sputtered to life, Matt stood and gave him a long big-brother look. He didn't say anything more, though, and they both got back to work.

Around three o'clock, Tucker took off toward the road, and Amanda heard the rumble of a school bus stopping at the end of the driveway. The clothes she'd borrowed from Marianne didn't fit well, and it had finally hit her that she was completely out of her element. Feeling like Dorothy after landing in Oz, she was more than a little anxious about how the afternoon would turn out.

"Here they are," she murmured, pulling a pitcher of fruit punch out of the fridge to go with the chocolate chip cookies she'd made. "I hope they like me."

"They will."

When she heard Marianne's voice, Amanda felt her cheeks warm with embarrassment. "Sorry. When I'm nervous, I talk to myself. Should you be up?"

"I have to go to the bathroom occasionally. Besides, I want to introduce you to the kids."

Amanda smiled. "Southern hospitality. I didn't realize how much I missed it."

"Things move a little more quickly in Los Angeles, I'd imagine." Grasping the arms, she eased herself into the chair at the head of the table. "I hope you won't be too bored here in Harland."

To be honest, Amanda was looking forward to some peace and quiet. She feared that saying so would open the door to a lot of questions, so she went with something less personal.

"Don't you worry about me. If you decide to hire me, this place will keep me plenty busy." When Marianne smiled, Amanda asked, "Did I say something funny?"

"No, but you've only been here a few hours and your accent's already coming back."

Apparently, she'd noticed earlier that Amanda had abandoned her Carolina drawl for something more mainstream. "I'd really rather not talk about it."

That got her a warm, understanding smile. "Okay. But when you're ready, I'm a good listener with a short memory."

Amanda wasn't sure she'd ever willingly discuss her situation, but right now a boy and girl stood framed in the screen door, gawking at her.

"Come on in, you two," their mother beckoned with a wave of her hand. "Meet an old friend of ours, Amanda Gardner. This is Kyle, who's twelve, and Emily, our eight-year-old."

"Nice to meet you," he said with a grin full of braces. The rubber bands holding them on were blue and gold. Harland Wildcats colors, she recalled with a smile of her own.

"Thanks." She shook the hand he boldly offered. "Nice to meet you, too."

Emily hung back a step behind her brother, eyeing Amanda with curiosity shining in china-blue eyes, just like her mother's. "You were in that commercial we saw with the animals stuck on an island during a flood. You and a bunch of other people saved them and found new homes for them."

The ad for a local SPCA group had been one of Amanda's favorite projects, and the mention of it gave her an ideal topic to break the ice with the kids.

"Usually I only got to do the boring stuff on commercials, so I had a ball making that one." She hunkered down so she was more on Emily's level. "One of those ponies used to steal my lunch if I wasn't careful. He really liked barbecue potato chips."

"What was his name?" Emily asked, clearly hooked.

"Constantine. He was the little black-and-white pinto. We called him Tino. He lives on a ranch in Montana, and next month he'll be in a big movie." That promotional campaign had been the last one she'd worked on before her world caved in, and she was clinging to that success for all she was worth. It kept her from feeling like a complete failure.

"I'd really like to see it," Emily said.

"Me, too." She almost added that they could go to the theater together, but she was afraid to sound presumptuous. After all, she didn't officially have this job yet. Standing, she put the plate of cookies on the table and filled two glasses with punch. "Are you guys hungry?"

"Starving," Kyle responded in typical boy fashion. Even though she knew he wasn't related to Ridge, he instantly reminded her of his stepfather. Forthright and confident, with a quick smile. Half the girls in town probably had crushes on this kid.

Pleased with how their first meeting had gone, she sat down and listened while they told Marianne about their day. School would be finished soon, and then they'd be home for the summer. With the twins due in July or August, it would be a busy time for the family.

And possibly for her, too. It sure would beat wringing her hands, waiting for another anvil to fall on her head, she mused as she broke off a quarter of a cookie.

"You don't have to do that." Kyle nodded toward the partial cookie she held. "There's plenty. You can have a whole one."

"Oh, this is fine. I don't eat a lot of sweets." When the two of them stared at her as if she'd been transported in from another planet, she decided it was best to play along. Picking up the rest of the cookie, she grinned. "But these are really good, if I do say so myself."

"Amanda's going to be here the next few days, to see if she'd like to help us out while I'm resting," Marianne explained. "If we all agree, we'll ask her to stay."

"I like her, Mommy," Emily chirped sweetly. "I've always wanted a big sister."

Kyle was eyeing her curiously, and Amanda decided to take a shot. "What about you? Think we can get along?"

"Sure. Can my buddies meet you?"

"As our *friend*," his mother insisted. "I know Amanda's very pretty, but the last thing she needs is a herd of twelve-year-old boys camped out on the porch, staring through the windows at her."

Kyle's shoulders slumped, but he mumbled some kind of agreement. Feeling sorry for him, Amanda leaned over and whispered, "They can stare a little. I don't mind."

That perked him up, and they fist-bumped to seal their deal. After a few more minutes, Marianne excused herself to go to the bathroom, artfully leaving the three of them to get better acquainted. To Amanda's tremendous relief, it went well. Before long she was helping Emily study for tomorrow's math test and listening to

Kyle run through a list of key dates in the American Revolution.

As poorly as the day had started, it was ending on a very positive note. Maybe, she thought hopefully, this was a sign of better things to come.

You needed an engineering degree to run this space-age washing machine.

Muttering to herself, Amanda reread the instructions for the third time and tapped the touch screen, but all she could do was make it spin. No water, no agitator, just spin. Having relied on a service for years, she was sorely out of practice in the laundry department. Determined to figure things out, she glowered at the control panel, as if she could scare it into cooperating.

Finally, she found the right combination of settings, and water flowed into the tub. She whooped in triumph, then halted mid-celebration. Had she already added the soap? She vaguely recalled hearing a receptionist at her old office complain about using too much detergent in her fancy new washing machine and having to pay a technician to clean it out.

Sighing in frustration, Amanda waited impatiently, tapping her foot until bubbles appeared in the water. It wasn't graceful or easy, but she managed to get a couple of loads done and dried that evening. The prize was that she'd be able to wear her own clothes tomorrow.

It was almost dark when John and Ridge came through the kitchen door, covered in dust and sweat. Without a single word, John headed straight into the downstairs bathroom.

"Don't mind him," Ridge advised wearily. "He's mad 'cause he had to walk in from that farthest back field when his tractor quit again. How's it going in here?" He nodded at the piles of laundry spread across the counter.

She'd never admit how much trouble the simple task had caused her, so she smiled. "Oh, fine. I'm just trying to keep everyone's clothes straight."

"There's a lot to do," he commented with a frown. "Sorry about that."

"No problem." After all, the more work there was, the more they needed her. "Is Matt with you guys?"

"No, he went home a couple hours ago to take over baby duty. Hailey's been pretty fussy lately, and he wanted to give Caty a break."

"Pretty soon, that'll be you. Two babies will keep you and Marianne pretty busy."

"You got that right. Could I talk to you about something?" He motioned her to a seat at the table.

Nothing good had ever happened to her after an intro like that, but Amanda tamped down her anxiety and tried to look calm as they sat down. "Sure."

Folding his hands on the table, he gave her a wry grin. "That didn't come out well, did it?"

"That depends," she hedged. "What did you mean to say?"

"Marianne and the kids think you're perfect for us. Even Tucker, from what I hear. I'm pretty easy to please, but I want to be absolutely clear about something." Amanda prompted him to continue, and he glanced over his shoulder before leaning in to speak more quietly. "I don't want Marianne left alone, not even for a few minutes. She'll insist she can manage on her own for a little while. She might even pull rank on you and make it an order."

"She doesn't like being laid up like this," Amanda added to show she understood. "Besides that, she's used to being in charge."

"Exactly. Plus, she thinks of you like another little sister, and I'm assuming you feel the same way. If she thinks she can do the mom thing on you, she will."

Amanda leaned in with a determined look. "She can try all she wants, but it won't work with me. I've been swimming with sharks for years, and she's got nothing on them."

Sitting back, Ridge studied her with a thoughtful expression. Even though she knew it was stupid, she actually held her breath, wondering what kind of decision he'd reach.

When he offered her a large, scarred hand, her pulse kicked up eagerly. She waited a beat before responding. "You're already convinced you want me to stay?"

"Did you mean what you said?"

"Absolutely. Fudging only leads to trouble, and I'm not looking for any more of that."

"Good to know." Shaking her hand, he stood and said, "Now I'm gonna go enjoy a little Disney time with my family. Good night."

"Night, Ridge."

She watched him stroll into the living room where Marianne and the kids were lounging on the bed, watching some hilarious cartoon. That such an obviously masculine guy could enjoy a children's show surprised Amanda, and she couldn't help smiling. Listening to them talking and laughing gave her a warm, cozy feeling, and she silently thanked the Collinses for offering her a lifeline when she needed one so badly.

That thought led her to John and his frosty attitude toward her. Would he ever forgive her for ignoring him all these years? She hoped so. The past few months, her so-called friends had deserted her, one by one. None had turned out to be who she thought they were, and she'd reluctantly come to realize she was better off without them.

John was an entirely different story, though. He was the same strong, solid guy she remembered, and more. Regaining his respect would be a huge step in the direction she wanted her life to go.

When the bathroom door opened and he came out, she adopted a friendly expression. "Hungry?"

"Not really." Moving to the pocket doors, he eased them closed and swiveled to face her. "We should get your car off the road."

Amanda frowned. "Wouldn't it be easier to do it in the daylight?"

"Yeah, but if someone notices it and calls Marianne, she'll freak about your driving all this way from California in a car that pretty much exploded."

"I see your point." When she grabbed her keys, he laughed. "What's so funny?"

"I ain't gonna drive it. I'll tow it in with a tractor while you steer and put on the brakes when I tell you to."

His condescending tone grated on her already fragile nerves. It made her think of the way he'd handled Ginger the Airhead, and she didn't appreciate it at all. Amanda had to tilt her head back to look him squarely in the eyes, but she glared up at him for all she was worth. "I'm not an idiot. You don't have to talk to me like I'm still four."

"Y'know," he muttered with a glare of his own, "we just might be mature enough for kindergarten."

"I am," she assured him airily, buffing her ragged fingernails on her T-shirt. "I'm not sure about you, though."

Grimacing, he dragged his fingers through his damp hair and gave her a long, exasperated look. "You still get to me, Gardner. I just wish I knew why."

Amanda's heart leapt at the thought that, despite her nagging fears, she might be able to mend her relationship with John. In Hollywood, she'd learned to strictly control her true feelings because being naive could easily derail the career she'd fought so hard to build. But tonight, standing in this homey kitchen with him, she eased up on those reins.

"You still get to me, too, Sawyer." Since that didn't seem like enough, she added a warm smile. "Now let's go get my car out of sight before it causes you any trouble."

John opened the screen door and followed her outside. Slipping his hands into his back pockets, he said, "If we're gonna be around each other all the time, we have to figure out a way to get along."

"I'll be nice if you will."

Slanting a look over at her, he flashed a crooked grin. "Deal."

"See? That wasn't so hard."

Inside the barn, he climbed onto a tractor and shifted to the far side of the seat. When she gave him a quizzical look, he said, "It's a ways out there. You riding or walking?"

"Oh, right." She pulled herself up, prepared to sit next to him the way she had when they were younger. She'd always loved riding around with him, bouncing over the plowed rows, laughing and not worrying about anything but holding on tightly to him.

Tonight, though, the seat looked way too small for the two of them to share. To keep things respectable, she perched on the metal step and grabbed on to an upright support with both hands. "Ready."

Chuckling, he shook his head but didn't say anything about her being ridiculous. He started the engine, fiddling with the throttle until the motor settled into a steady rumble. He took a straight course over the fields, and the first bump made Amanda yelp in surprise. He must have heard her, but instead of slowing down, he went faster.

Typical John, she thought, rolling her eyes.

When they reached her car, he dialed the tractor down to idle, and the sound died enough for conversation.

"Thanks for going so slow," she teased as they both jumped down.

Sending her a mischievous grin, he lifted a chain from the equipment box mounted behind his seat. He slid under the back of her car, and she heard clanking as he wrapped the chain around the axle. More clanking, then a muffled, "What's it like?"

At first, she didn't know what he meant. After a few dense seconds, she caught on. "You mean L.A.?"

"Yeah."

"It's gorgeous, and there's always tons of stuff going on, so it's really exciting to live there. Malibu is breathtaking, looking out over the ocean like that."

Sliding free, he stood and brushed off his jeans. "I've seen it on TV," he said as he tightened some kind of holder through two of the chain's links. "Real nice. Is that where you live?"

"Lived," she corrected him wistfully. "In an adorable beach house a stone's throw from the water. Until I lost my job and couldn't pay the rent. Landlords don't like that."

Leaning back against her car, John frowned. "I don't get it. There must be other PR and advertising firms you could have worked for. Why didn't you stay there and get another job?"

"I couldn't."

"Why?"

John had echoed the question she'd asked herself hundreds of times while her meticulously plotted life had unraveled around her. That he was standing here with her in the near-darkness, helping with her wrecked car, was the final straw.

After keeping it together for weeks, Amanda burst into tears.

Chapter Three

Even Superman had his weakness, John reasoned as he instinctively took Amanda in his arms. For him, it was a woman's tears. They always reduced him to a helpless state, where he could think of only one thing: make them stop.

"It's okay, Panda," he soothed as she burrowed into his chest. "You're home now. Everything's gonna be fine."

He'd used her old nickname hoping to make her feel better, but it only made her cry harder. She was trying to say something, but between the sniffling and the sobbing, he couldn't make out a single word. So he stood there like a moron, just holding her, praying she'd blow herself out and calm down enough to tell him what was so wrong.

After a few agonizing minutes, she got herself together, pulling away with a final sniff. When she moved to wipe her cheeks with hands grimy from the tractor, he caught them in his. His intent was to keep her from getting grease all over her face, but the result of his impulsive move hit him like a sucker punch.

Damp cheeks glistening in the sunset, she gazed up at him with a look that was a heart-stopping mix of sorrow and gratitude. She brought to mind a stray kitten who wanted nothing more than to be picked up and cuddled. It would have been so easy to lean in and kiss her, and John came dangerously close to doing just that.

Startled, he stepped back to put some space between them. His arms felt empty without her, but he firmly shoved the impression away and focused on keeping his distance. And his good-guy status.

"Sorry about that," she murmured. "I know you hate it when girls cry."

"Most guys do, 'cause we don't know how to make you stop."

With a wan smile, she patted his arm. "You did just fine, but if I don't get that laundry into the drier, no one will have any clean towels tomorrow. We should get this car tucked away."

"Soon as you tell me what set you off, we'll go."

When she hesitated, he folded his arms and waited.

"John, I'm exhausted. Could we please put off the third degree until morning?"

"You'll tell me everything? No more secrets?"

"Yes." He cocked his head, and she sighed. "Promise."

"Okay, then."

She hadn't noticed his bizarre reaction to her, John thought while he opened the driver's door and closed it behind her. As he swung onto the tractor and increased the throttle, he counted himself fortunate to escape with his male dignity intact.

No doubt about it, he still had a very soft spot for Amanda Gardner. He'd have to watch his step.

John came through the door around six the next morning, drawn by the prospect of breakfast. The sun peeking over the hills was all he needed to get him in gear, but he knew Matt, Ridge and their farmhands would appreciate the coffee already brewing. The stainless-steel, commercial-grade coffeemaker was steaming away, filling one pot on the bottom while another waited on top.

Then he realized something was wrong. The smell wasn't as strong as usual. When he noticed the pot was filled with mostly water, he got up to remedy the problem.

As he was pulling the container from the cupboard, he heard, "What are you doing?"

Without turning, he pressed the pause button

and started scooping grounds into the empty filters. "Adding coffee to your coffee."

Amanda muttered something very unladylike. "You're kidding."

"Nope. Sorry."

When he turned to face her, he felt his jaw start to drop and had to remind himself to keep his mouth closed. She'd obviously washed her own clothes last night.

Dressed in faded jeans and a pink tank, she looked like she was ready for a picnic, not a day of housework. Her damp, curly hair was pulled up into a bouncy ponytail, a few stray pieces framing those incredible eyes. The war paint was gone, and her face had that fresh-as-a-daisy quality he'd missed yesterday.

He'd known his fair share of blonde, blue-eyed women, preferred them actually. But none of them had ever matched the one standing only a few feet away. He'd thought his imagination had idealized her over the years, making her seem more beautiful than she'd actually been. Seeing her now proved that he'd remembered every detail of her perfectly.

Amanda was watching him, holding the kids' lunch boxes in her hands. She didn't look scared, but she didn't look confident, either. John knew how she felt. Considering their spontaneous embrace last night, he was beginning to have serious doubts about her staying at the farm.

Seeing her this way wasn't helping any.

"Thanks for the help. I guess I'm not quite awake," she confided with a dainty yawn.

"No problem." Backing away to cover his discomfort, he nodded at the coffeemaker. "Some of that will help."

"Oh, I don't drink it anymore."

John couldn't believe his ears. In high school, she'd been a total caffeine hound. "Since when?"

"It's been a while now." She cast a longing look at the filling pot, then turned away to get some plates out of the cupboard. "Waffles are warming in the oven, and there's fresh strawberries. Would you like some?"

John felt odd having her wait on him as if he was at a restaurant instead of in his sister's kitchen. "Sure, but I'll get 'em. You've got enough to do getting the kids ready for school."

"Okay."

While she pulled lunch supplies out of the cupboard, he heaped a plate with waffles. "This is kinda weird, huh? Your working here, I mean," he added to be clear. He didn't want her thinking he was up all night wondering what had brought her here. He hadn't thought about it. Much.

Shrugging, she started spreading peanut butter onto sandwiches. "A little."

"Well, don't feel like you have to wait on us or anything," he advised as he sat down. "We all know where everything is."

Glancing over, she narrowed her eyes. "Meaning I don't?"

Sensing he'd unintentionally touched a nerve, John sat back, hands in the air. "Meaning nothing. We're just not the type of folks who have a housekeeper is all."

"And I am, is that it?"

"Well, aren't you?" Sensing they were headed for an argument they'd both regret, he tried to defuse it with a grin. "I mean, you can't even make coffee."

She didn't even try to zing him back, and started hunting through the cupboards for something. He could have asked what she wanted, but after the slap down he'd gotten, he wasn't inclined to be helpful just now.

Touchy, John thought as he pawed through the newspaper for the sports section. When he glanced over and caught her observing him, her disapproving frown told him she didn't like the way he'd fanned the paper out across the table. Well, too bad. He'd done that every morning of his life since his father had taught him how to read the baseball box scores. He wasn't about to change just because some uptight California girl didn't like a mess.

As she reached into the fridge for drink boxes, she said, "I'm sorry for jumping down your throat."

"It's okay. You'll feel better once you get the hang of things."

"I thought my PR job was tough," she confessed while she plucked grapes and dropped them into small plastic containers. "But I only had to worry about my clients and myself, and I had plenty of help. Keeping a family going is a thousand times harder. I don't know how Marianne does it."

"Experience," John replied. "Don't forget, she got a lot of practice with me."

Amanda laughed, and in view of the rocky start their morning had gotten off to, John considered that a major improvement.

"Those pocket doors between the kitchen and living room are really nice," she went on in a much more pleasant tone. "When did you add those?"

"The slots have always been there, but the doors were in the attic. Matt and I put them up last weekend to give Marianne and Ridge some privacy. They're solid oak, so they keep out a lot of noise, too. Lets Marianne rest when she needs it."

Dropping the drinks and grapes into each bag, Amanda glanced over at him. "You're really worried about her, aren't you?"

John never mentioned it, since he was supposed to be the optimist in the family. But her sympathetic tone made him nod. "We all are. Twins are tough for anyone, and she's not twenty anymore. Just don't tell her I said that."

Smiling, Amanda gave him a broad wink. "I'm great at keeping secrets."

She sure was. It was driving him nuts, wondering what was going on. Before his good sense could talk him out of bringing it up, he said, "Speaking of secrets, you need to tell me what's going on."

"I drove out here from California and my car broke down," she answered while she filled the waffle iron with batter.

Cocking his head, he scowled. "And?"

Sighing, she closed the griddle and flashed him a hesitant look. "My parents know, but I'm not sure you want to hear it."

Folding his hands on the table, he gave her his full attention. "Try me."

She wet a dishcloth and started cleaning the counter. John knew perfectly well she was trying to avoid looking at him, but he let it go.

"About a year ago," she began, "this new executive joined our firm. Over drinks one night, he said he was divorced and interested in dating me. We were together about six months before Ted finally told me he was still technically married."

"Ted who?"

Shaking her head, she gave him an I-know-what-you're-doing smile.

"Don't want me going after him, huh?" John asked.

"Bingo."

"Answer me one thing. How can someone be 'technically' married?"

"His words, not mine," she explained. "Anyway, when I found out, I broke things off. But we were quite an item, so everybody knew about us, and most of them knew he was married. The whole thing was humiliating. As if that wasn't enough, one Monday we got to the office and the doors were locked. They were glass, and we could see the whole place was empty."

"You're kidding."

"Totally serious," she responded with a sour expression. "We discovered the company was bankrupt, and the owners had sold off everything that wasn't nailed down."

"Just like that? Don't they have to give you notice or something?"

"Well, they didn't."

Bad as all this sounded, her brittle tone alerted John that he hadn't heard the worst of it. "Something else happened to send you running back here. What was it?"

Another sigh, this one so deep it made his chest

ache. "My accountant had some financial problems of his own, and his solution was to borrow—" she added air quotes "—the money from me. The trouble was, he couldn't pay it back. Long story short, I'm beyond broke. I auctioned off everything I could, but it wasn't enough to pay off the debts I didn't know had been piling up over the last two years."

"That's stealing," John pointed out. "Shouldn't they have put him behind bars or something?"

Anger flared in her eyes, giving them more life than he'd seen the whole time she'd been back. "Trust me, if we could have found him, he'd be in jail." As quickly as it had spiked, the spirit ebbed away. "The closest we got was hearing he might have gone to Brazil. The problem is, tracking someone down costs money, and I didn't have any."

"That explains why you're driving that car." Hoping to lighten the mood, he copied her by air-quoting the final word. His attempt earned him a wan smile, but it was better than nothing.

"After a lot of thought, I decided that I'd made every mistake a person possibly could, and I needed a complete change of scenery. Lifestyle-wise and geographically, Harland was as far from L.A. as I could get." Now, she pinned him with a begging look. "Don't tell Marianne and Ridge. They'll think I'm a brainless idiot, and I really need this job. I had to declare bankruptcy, so I've got nothing but the clothes in my duffel bag."

Being a farmer, John was well acquainted with the concept of bankruptcy. While the Sawyers had escaped it themselves, many of their neighbors hadn't been so fortunate. That Amanda had been forced to endure that harsh penalty through no fault of her own made him want to help her get back on her feet.

But he was a simple, straightforward guy. By his own example, Ethan had taught all of them that honesty wasn't just the best way, it was the only way. John had taken his father's lesson to heart as a child, and it was the compass that kept his life on its normally smooth, easygoing path.

Amanda's situation presented him with a difficult choice. Either respect her wishes and keep his family in the dark, or tell them the truth and let Marianne make her own judgment.

Or he could convince Amanda to tell them herself. Not only would it force everything out in the open, it would enable her to dust herself off and make plans for her future. Of course, with the very headstrong Amanda Gardner, that was easier said than done.

His silence must have started to worry her. "Please, John? It's been a long time since something went right for me."

Hoping to appear unconcerned, he grinned. "I can have blueberry pancakes whenever I want?"

"Absolutely," she breathed with a grateful smile. "Then it's a deal."

He still had his misgivings, but after all she'd been through, knowing he could make her smile made him feel incredible.

The shifting emotions on John's face had been simple enough for Amanda to read. Wariness when he saw her in the kitchen that morning. Concern for his sister and her babies. Then something darker that had no place shadowing his wide-open features.

John was as different from the other men she'd known as the sun was from the moon. Over the years, she'd thought about her rugged country boy many times, wondering what he was doing, if he was happy. Now he was right in front of her, and she could see for herself how much he enjoyed his sweet, simple life.

Get up at the crack of dawn, have breakfast with your family, work hard all day, play with the kids and the dog, go to sleep, repeat. Oh, and save the occasional damsel in distress. All of that flitted through her head in a heartbeat, and she realized she'd forgotten to do something very important yesterday.

"John?" When his eyes met hers, she gulped

down her pride and rushed on. "I want to thank you for all your help. You've been really great."

"You're welcome."

For a fleeting moment, the twinkle she recalled so fondly lit his eyes. She was asking a lot, but she knew she could count on him to keep her secret. Then the suspicious look returned. "There's something else. What is it?"

Her heart thudded to a stop, and she berated herself for assuming she was in the clear. Perceptive as he was, she should have known better. Luckily for her, the kids chose that precise moment to come rushing downstairs for breakfast. They could work in showbiz, she thought with a grin. They had impeccable timing.

"Waffles!" Kyle shouted before John got his attention with a finger over his lips. "Sorry," he said more quietly, turning to Amanda. "But I really love waffles. Are they burning?"

"Oh, no!" She'd forgotten all about them during her talk with John, and the griddle was smoking in protest. She flipped it open and used a towel to fan the smoke toward the open window. "Sorry, guys. I'll make more."

"Not for me," Emily mumbled. "I don't feel good."

John's frown alerted Amanda that his niece wasn't the kind of kid who tried to dodge school with fake tummy aches. Resting a hand on the girl's forehead, Amanda frowned, too. "That's a fever, missy. No school for you."

The pocket doors slid open, and Marianne entered the kitchen, apparently drawn by some inexplicable maternal instinct. "Not feeling too well, Emmy?"

"No." Her lip quivered, and Marianne opened her arms wide. Looking miserable, Emily shook her head. "I don't want to make you and the babies sick."

"You won't."

"Are you sure?"

"A hundred percent." Marianne sat down on the bench near the table. "Mommies know these things."

She patted the seat beside her, and Emily cautiously joined her. When Marianne pulled her close, she snuggled in, closing her eyes as if everything was suddenly right with the world. Ridge appeared in the doorway and kissed the top of his daughter's head before turning to Kyle.

"I've gotta get some things at the hardware store," he said. "If you want, we can grab breakfast at Ruthy's Place, then you can help me pick up what I need. When we're done, I'll drop you off at school."

The boy grabbed his backpack, eyes bright with excitement. "Okay."

"Ridge, you must be really busy," Amanda

said. "I can take Kyle to school if you'll just loan me your car."

Ridge traded a grin with his son. "Thanks, but we like to get some guy time once in a while, don't we?"

"Sure do."

"Just make sure he's on time for his first class," Marianne warned. "I don't want to get another message from the attendance office and have to call all over town hunting for you two."

"We'll either be at Ruthy's or Harland Hardware." Ridge paused to kiss her as he and Kyle headed for the door. "Not hard."

"Or the fairgrounds watching them bull-doze the dirt track, or at the airport watching the planes take off and land, or—" She was still talking when the screen door slammed shut behind them. Sighing, she pulled Emily in for a quick hug. "Those boys. What on earth will we do with them?"

"Boys are nothing but trouble, Mommy. I'm glad one of our babies is a girl."

Smiling, Marianne broke a couple of pieces from John's untouched waffles for her daughter. "Just eat a little bit, then we'll give you something to get that fever down."

Reaching into the cupboard, Amanda handed a bottle of children's fever medicine to Marianne.

That was when she noticed Kyle's lunch still sitting on the counter. She'd lost count of the mistakes she'd made this morning, and it was only six-thirty. "I'll take Kyle's lunch to school later. What time does he eat?"

Marianne waved the idea away. "Don't worry about it. He has a lunch account, so he can buy today. If he's got any appetite left after the farmer's breakfast Ruthy will feed him, that is."

"Are you sure?"

"Definitely," her new boss assured her. "You look a little stressed. Sit down and have something to eat."

Touched by the concern, Amanda smiled. It was so nice to have someone looking out for her, instead of constantly fending for herself and pretending fate hadn't buried her in an avalanche of failure.

She poured herself a glass of orange juice and sat down at the table with a bowl of fruit. Hoping to reroute her morning onto a better track, she chose a pleasant topic. "So, you're expecting a boy and a girl. Do you have names picked out yet?"

"Andrew Ethan, and Chelsea Ann," Emily replied proudly. "We all picked our favorite names and mixed them together."

"What a fabulous idea." She glanced over at John. "How do you like being an uncle?"

"It's great. I get all the fun and none of the responsibility."

"You and Uncle Matt are the best uncles in the whole world," Emily informed him. "We love you to pieces."

Recognizing the phrase, Amanda smiled at Marianne. "She sounds like you."

"Well, I don't say it often," she commented, handing her daughter a small pill. "When I do, I really mean it."

After obediently taking her medicine, the princess of the family gazed hopefully at her mother. "Can we watch *Cinderella?*"

"Again?" John groaned. "We just watched it the other night. Twice."

"It's my favorite."

"This week, anyway."

"You can pick next time," she promised, getting a quick grin in reply.

"Sounds good." Pushing off from the table, he stood and took a pair of work gloves from the shelf near the door. "Enjoy your day, ladies. Once I fix our beast of a tractor, I'm hoping to get started on that new field today."

"Do you want something for lunch?" Marianne asked.

Amanda mentally kicked herself for not thinking of that. She should have asked Ridge, too.

"Nah. If I get hungry, I'll wander back in."

"They're predicting rain today," Amanda warned.

He shrugged as if it was no big deal. "God's in charge of the weather. I just work with what He gives me."

Kissing Marianne's cheek and ruffling Emily's hair, he glanced at Amanda briefly before strolling out the door. The other two decided it was movie time and headed into the living room, leaving Amanda alone with her breakfast.

While she munched on a piece of cantaloupe, Amanda watched John through the screen. As his long, easy strides took him toward the equipment barn, Amanda was struck by how different he was from the boy she'd known. Back then, he'd been a free spirit, and nothing had seemed to faze him. Now he worried, and despite his claim to have no responsibilities, it hadn't taken her long to discover that was hardly the case. He had many, and he took them very seriously.

But some things—the most important ones—hadn't changed a bit. His comment about the weather reminded her how strong his faith had always been. Trusting in God seemed to give him an even-keeled perspective she envied. Devoted to his family, John had never lived anywhere but this farm, and she wouldn't be surprised to learn that he wanted to be buried here, too. In between, he'd work his family's land, devoting his considerable energy to whatever task needed to be done.

Because that was the kind of guy he was. Grounded and content, not looking over the horizon, longing for something more. He'd been born into the life he was meant to live, and it suited him perfectly. While Amanda had restlessly pursued one dream after another, not once had she considered doing things differently.

Now that her splashy dreams had come crashing down around her, she couldn't help wondering if she'd chosen the wrong path.

Putting in this new field just might be the end of him.

John slid the newly repaired engine into idle to cool it down. They hadn't planted anything on this section of the farm since it flooded five years ago. In one sense that was good. The soil was well-rested and ready for crops. On the other hand, it was awful because the field grass had taken over, plunging its roots deep into the ground and wrapping around anything in its way.

As if that wasn't bad enough, the receding creek had left behind hundreds of rocks. They appeared where he least expected them, forcing him to get down and toss them free by hand when the plow couldn't move them aside. At this rate he wouldn't have time to plant anything here until next season.

With those dark thoughts crowding each other in his mind, John climbed back up and moved the tractor along. In his imagination, he heard his father's voice, wisely reminding him he had two choices. He could either give up or keep trying.

After some serious internal debate, he kept working because quitting just didn't sit right with him.

At around one, the gray clouds that had been steadily advancing all day started grumbling with thunder. Normally, he would have grumbled right along, but today the storm was a relief. He was exhausted from his poor night's sleep and a long morning of tedious work. In all honesty, he thought as he drove back to the equipment barn, he was ready for a nice, long nap.

He didn't know what was wrong with him. As he shut the engine down, he tried to remember the last time he'd had trouble sleeping. This time of year, most evenings he was so beat he dropped off as soon as he stretched out somewhere even remotely comfortable. He'd once spent an entire night snoozing on the front porch swing because he sat down to take off his boots and couldn't go another step.

He managed not to look over at Amanda's tarp-covered wreck in the corner, knowing it would only make matters worse. Glad to leave his frustrations behind for a while, he battled the wind to slide the barn door closed. When he heard a frustrated scream, he turned to see what was up.

Amanda was fighting the storm herself, struggling to pull a large quilt off the clothesline while it billowed out like a sail. Hustling over, he grabbed one end and held it steady while she yanked the clothespins free.

A little out of breath, she thanked him. "For a few seconds there, I thought it was going to take off with me."

"It's the least I could do, seeing as this is mine."

She gave him a look usually reserved for horror films. "It was covered in mud and other things I'd rather not think about. What did you do? Sleep in your boots?"

He laughed. "Nah. Tucker and I had a sleepover a couple nights ago. It was late, and I didn't check him over before he jumped up on my bed. I think he spent the day in the swamp."

"You shouldn't let him in your house without hosing him off first."

"You sound like Marianne," he teased. "It's just dirt. No harm done."

"I guess." Folding the quilt into a large square, she handed it to him. "Here you go."

"Thanks."

It was awkward, standing there staring at each other. Amanda glanced around, then focused on something down the lane. "Marianne said you live in the old carriage house we played in when we were kids."

Even though Amanda had only been there a day, she'd blended into the farm's routine so seamlessly that he'd forgotten how long she'd been gone. His instincts told him that meant something, but he didn't want to think about it now, so he ignored the message.

"When Marianne and the kids moved back here, they needed space in the main house. We fixed up the carriage house for me."

"Could I see it?"

"Sure."

John shrugged, hoping to give the impression it didn't matter one way or the other. Actually, as they walked down the path toward his small front porch, he was trying to remember if he'd collected his week's worth of dirty clothes or if they were still in piles next to his unmade bed.

Opening the door, he bit back a groan. The place was a disaster, and he could almost hear Marianne scolding him for inviting poor, unsuspecting company into a pigsty. To his surprise, Amanda started laughing.

"You're still a slob, Sawyer. It's nice to know some things never change."

From the merriment dancing in her eyes, she meant it, so he laughed along with her. "Yeah, well, it works for me."

Moving inside, she assessed his home with an appreciative look. "This is great. I love how you left the old beams alone and worked around them." Tipping her head back, she asked, "How high is this ceiling?"

"Fourteen feet," he answered proudly. "There's another twelve feet of headroom upstairs."

She rested a hand on the crude ladder that led to his attic. "What's up there?"

"Nothing. It's for later, when I want to expand."

"Expand?" she echoed, curiosity lighting those gorgeous eyes. "For what?"

Busted. Trapped in his own words, John decided there was no harm in laying out his plans for her. "There's enough space for a couple bedrooms and a bathroom up there. Then it would be a nice place for a family. Y'know, someday."

"You could put in a garden and patio out back." She pointed through the French doors that framed his view of the pond like an old painting. "It would be really pretty."

That was exactly what he had in mind, and he was impressed that she'd matched his thoughts so easily. Then again, anyone could have done the same. The picture-perfect landscape outside his unused kitchen called out for enjoying. These days, he just didn't have the time.

Scoping out his digs, Amanda paused near the shelves that hung next to his door. His collection of trophies took up most of the space, but in the front, right where he could always see it, was something more valuable to him than all the shiny hardware he'd accumulated in high school.

Taken at a church event in the square, the faded photo showed all six Sawyers on a checked blanket, enjoying one of the many picnics they'd shared. Only this one was special. A few months later, his mother had passed away from leukemia. It was the last picture of them all together, and his brother and sisters had their own framed copies. Wanting to preserve the moment forever, Lisa had painted an incredible version of it that now held the place of honor over the fireplace in the main house.

Amanda touched the shelf but not the frame, as if she sensed how precious it was. "You all looked so happy that day."

"Yeah, we did."

"Do you ever miss your mom?"

"I was only five when she died, so I don't remember much. Mostly that she loved flowers and laughed a lot."

"That's nice."

There wasn't much to say after that. Putting

thoughts of the past aside, John flung the quilt out and let it fall onto his bed. "Much better. Thanks for washing it."

Hands on her hips, she angled her head in disapproval. "You can't be serious."

"What?"

Sighing as if he'd suggested she get a manicure at the tractor supply store, she pulled the quilt loose and set it on a chair stacked with issues of *Sports Illustrated* he hadn't had a chance to read. "Do you have any more sheets?"

"In the bathroom."

"You go get them while I strip these."

"You don't have to—" She gave him The Look, and he put up his hands in surrender. "Yes, ma'am."

"Good boy."

Pausing in the bathroom doorway, he turned back. "I don't remember your being this bossy."

"I wasn't, but I am now. Get over it."

As John rummaged in his linen closet for clean sheets, he couldn't decide if he liked the new Amanda or if she was going to drive him completely over the edge.

Chapter Four

"In your face, machine."

Thursday morning, Amanda punched the final button for the whites wash sequence, getting a muted hum in reply. After a celebratory fist pump, she checked on the drier and found it was only halfway through its cycle. It felt like she'd been doing laundry continuously since she'd arrived. The trouble wasn't the amount of clothes, towels and sheets, but the time gap between washing and drying. It took twice as long to dry each load as it did to wash it. At this rate, by the time she "finished" the laundry, there would be another pile waiting for her attention.

She really hated stacks of unfinished work.

Tapping her chin, she pondered whether there was a way to speed up the process and make it more efficient. She could try staggering the loads, or set the controls to run in the middle of the night. But then she'd have wet laundry first thing every morning, which wouldn't solve the problem of how to dry things faster.

While she was mulling over this problem, her eyes drifted toward the clothesline she'd used the other day to avoid ruining the batting in John's quilt. If she hung sheets out there, they could dry in the breeze while clothes and towels got the fluff treatment inside. That might work, she thought, lifting the basket of wet linens and heading out the side porch door.

In California, her yard had consisted of a ten-foot-square patio surrounded by walls and a smattering of potted plants that frequently died because she forgot to water them. Never mind hanging wash out on a line to soak up the fresh air.

Then again, she thought as she pinned the end of a fitted sheet to the line, Malibu's salt air wasn't the kind you'd want to bring inside. After she got the rest of the linens hung, she paused to look around. She'd caught herself doing that a lot, and she couldn't understand why. She'd grown up in Harland, and spent a lot of time at the Sawyer farm. It wasn't new to her, but for some reason it felt that way.

Maybe it was her perspective, she mused. Maybe it was the fact that her new job—thank you, Marianne—gave her time to stop and appreciate her surroundings. That thought made her smile when she noticed the dust cloud in a far-off field. John was out there, pounding big rocks into smaller rocks, he'd joked. It was only ten, and already the thermometer registered eighty-seven in the sun.

That field was all sun, she realized on her way inside. Matt and Ridge had been in earlier for a break, but not John. He was making up time after yesterday's washout, and she wouldn't be surprised if he worked right through lunch. If she let him.

She piled ham and cheese onto a sandwich then filled a large thermos with sweet tea and dropped some oatmeal cookies still warm from the oven into a bag. Just as her foot hit the bottom porch step, Tucker zoomed around the corner of the house, yapping and racing in circles.

He was so enthusiastic, she couldn't keep back a laugh. "Oh, no. I'm not racing. You can come along, though."

That seemed to be enough for him, and he ran ahead, checking over his shoulder several times to make sure she was still following. *What a great dog,* she thought with a grin. *Every kid should have a pet like that.*

It was a long walk out to where John was slaving away, and she figured there was no rush since he wasn't expecting her. For the first time in forever, she didn't hurry. While her days were busy, once the kids were off to school, she didn't have a schedule to meet. There was always something that needed doing, but no one was standing over her, waiting for her to finish. Or emailing or texting or calling to find out when she'd be someplace or other. Or waiting to stab her in the back.

Instead, she strolled along the dusty field road, admiring the daisies and day lilies and dozens of other wildflowers that blended into the earthy scent of this sunny morning. Dragonflies and bumblebees zoomed around her, pausing for a second or two on their way to wherever they were going. At one point, a hummingbird hovered in front of her, as if checking her out.

As he raced off, Amanda realized she was smiling. She'd been anxious about making the transition from big city to sleepy hometown, thinking she'd miss all the excitement she'd come to enjoy so much. Turned out she'd been worrying over nothing. After only a few days in Harland, L.A. was quickly fading into the past.

When she reached the field John was working on, he didn't notice her at first. With the tractor idling, he was using a long metal bar to pry a large rock from the ground. Grunting with the effort, he finally managed to loosen it. Bending down, he wrestled it free and tossed it far into the woods.

"Nice try," he muttered, a little out of breath. When Amanda laughed, he turned with a surprised look that quickly became a sheepish grin. "Heard that, huh?"

"Yes." Holding up the snack she'd brought, she asked, "Ready for a break?"

Squinting up at the sun, he sighed. "Ten already. I'm way behind and it's like I haven't even started."

That he could nail the time without a watch impressed her. Just more evidence that she wasn't in L.A. anymore.

"Can I help somehow?" she asked as they both sat on the ground.

After a long swallow of tea, he shook his head. "Marianne shouldn't be by herself."

"She's not. She and Ridge were having a text argument about whether or not to paint the living room, so he finally came in to settle things."

"Lemme guess," John said with a knowing grin. "They're debating colors and curtains and stuff."

Amanda pointed at him as if he'd just won a game show. "Bingo. She's climbing the walls, so he decided to stay and keep her company for a while."

John gave her a long-suffering look. "That's my big sister. When she gets bored, she starts redecorating. We try to keep her busy."

"I'll see if I can come up with something for her to do while she's laid up."

"That'd be great."

Nibbling on a cookie, she glanced at the pile of rocks he'd built. "I could help for a while. If you want," she added to avoid insulting him. Some guys didn't like to admit they couldn't handle a job all on their own, and for all she knew he was one of them.

"I never turn down an extra set of hands." He motioned to the pile of rocks he'd tossed aside. "But they get kinda heavy."

"I could drive the tractor, then."

His laughter burst her little bubble, and she nearly gave up on the idea. But the old spirit she hadn't felt in months came to life inside her, and she tilted her nose in the air. "Just show me what to do, plowboy. I'm a quick study."

He quit laughing, but amusement still twinkled in his expressive eyes. "You're serious."

"How hard can it be?"

"The other night, you could barely hang on when I was driving."

Standing, she folded her arms and glared down at him. She normally had to look up at him, so this was an interesting vantage point. It also gave her the sensation of having the upper hand for a change. "Do you want my help or not? Because, trust me, I have plenty of other things I could be doing."

Shaking his head, he got to his feet and grinned at her. He didn't say anything, and she started to feel weird. "What?"

"It's nice to see that spunk of yours coming back is all." Reaching out, he flipped her ponytail with a grimy finger. "These curls are real pretty."

"I don't have time to dry my hair before breakfast," she said, suddenly very ill at ease. That was the teasing gesture she'd been hoping for when she arrived, but now that he'd done it, she felt strange.

"And all that war paint," he continued in a gentle, approving tone. "You look much better without it."

He hadn't moved, but for some insane reason she felt as if he'd gotten closer. Maybe it was the warm current under his drawl, or the appreciation gleaming in his eyes.

Or maybe, she thought in disgust, it was her very vivid imagination inventing something that had never—and would never—exist between them. They were friends—plain and simple. She'd just begun to rebuild the bridge she'd burned, and she wasn't about to do anything to send it crashing down again.

To cover her discomfort, she hopped onto the

tractor seat and gripped the metal steering wheel in her hands. "Show me what to do."

John demonstrated how to set the choke and adjust it to keep the cranky engine running. Having never driven anything other than an automatic transmission, she stalled it a few times before she got the hang of it. After that, she was able to control the speed so the plow could bite through the top layer of soil without straining the motor.

Glancing frequently over her shoulder, she saw John following closely, just off to the side. Whenever she turned over a rock bigger than a grapefruit, he'd motion for her to pause so he could reach in and throw it aside.

When the sun was directly overhead, he made a slashing movement across his throat. Figuring that meant to kill the engine, she shut the tractor down and looked to him for directions.

Looking around, he rested his hands on his hips with a satisfied expression. "Great job, Panda. We got way more done together than I did on my own."

His praise made her smile with pride. While it wasn't the easiest thing she'd ever taken on, it felt wonderful to pay back some of the kindness he'd shown her.

"I'm curious," she said as she stepped down

and joined him. "Why are you out here doing this all by yourself?"

"Well, it's my idea."

"What is?"

Turning toward the house, he began walking. "Soybeans."

Amanda's father had been a doctor, her mother a librarian. As a kid, she'd enjoyed hanging out at the farm, but knew absolutely nothing about farming. His answer might as well have been in a foreign language. "I'm a townie, Sawyer. I need a little more detail than that."

Chuckling, he explained. "We have to rotate our crops every few years, and I thought it might be good to get into something new. Over the winter, I went online to do some research about different things we could try here. Turns out soybeans are easy to grow and in demand all over the world."

She couldn't help smiling, and he scowled down at her. "What's so funny?"

"Did you just say, 'in demand'?"

"Yeah," he admitted with a sheepish grin. "Weird, huh?"

"Just a little." Linking arms with him, she gave a quick squeeze to let him know she was only razzing him. "So tell me what soybeans are used for."

"Vegetarians eat 'em, they're used in livestock

feed, soy milk, even biofuel. There's a great market for them right here in the States, and the distributor we use for our hay and corn told me he can't ever get enough to fill all his orders. I figured it was worth a shot."

"But Matt wasn't sure about it."

"You guessed it. But he was willing to let me try them, as long as they didn't gobble up any of the acreage we use for our other crops." He nodded at the rows they were strolling through. "I remembered this section out here and thought it'd be the perfect place to experiment."

"John Sawyer, agricultural visionary," she commented, only half teasing. When had her fun-loving buddy morphed into a risk-taking businessman? Then it hit her. "The farm's in financial trouble, isn't it?"

He sighed. "Always. We're treading water these days, but we've got a big loan to pay off later this year. We need more cash for that, so I'm praying this works."

In his tone, she heard more than a touch of concern, and she frowned. She'd endured her own slide into bankruptcy, but she'd only lost possessions, not a place. This farm meant so much to John and his family, she couldn't imagine what they'd do if things really went wrong.

Even though she wasn't sure she wanted to hear the answer, she asked, "What if it doesn't?"

"We'll have to sell off some acreage to make the payment. But that's the beginning of the end for a lot of farms, so Matt, Ridge and I are gonna try everything else first."

"Go, soybeans," she called out in her old cheerleader's voice, circling her arms into a V and ending with an impulsive deer jump.

That got her a bright laugh, and she congratulated herself on breaking him out of his uncharacteristic funk. As they went up the back porch steps, she asked, "What would you like for lunch?"

"Pancakes."

"Figures." Loony as his request was, she decided that as hard as he'd been working, he deserved a treat. "Blueberry or chocolate chip?"

Grinning like the boy she remembered so fondly, he opened the door for her. "Both."

One thing was for sure, John thought as a fluffy bite all but melted in his mouth. The woman knew her pancakes.

"Where'd you learn to make these things?" he asked Amanda while she spooned more onto the griddle.

"From a French pastry chef in Malibu. He had a little café, and I ate there a lot. Since I was such a good customer, he offered to share one of his recipes with me. I picked these."

"Good choice," he said with a grin. "For me, anyway."

"It's nice to be able to make them again. I wasn't sure I'd remember how."

Reference to her recent troubles dimmed the mood a little, and he tried to brighten things up again. "Trust me, Panda. You didn't forget a thing."

She gave him an odd look, even opened her mouth for a moment. Shutting it quickly, she turned away to take the batter bowl to the sink.

"Amanda?"

"Yes?"

"Something wrong?"

"No." Her back was still to him, and she ran water into the bowl. "Everything's fine."

John wasn't a brain surgeon, but he'd known enough women to sense when one was avoiding him. And that *Everything's fine* meant exactly the opposite.

He had no clue what was going on in that head of hers, but instinct told him it was important. Getting up from the table, he crossed the kitchen to stand behind her. When she still refused to face him, he gently spun her around.

The emotion flickering in her beautiful eyes was just a step shy of pain. That he might have done something to hurt her made his chest seize with regret, and he instinctively stepped closer. "What's wrong?"

Shrugging, she glanced away, but he tipped her chin up so she had to meet his eyes. The sadness he'd glimpsed deepened, darkening her eyes to a miserable grayish-blue.

"You call me Panda," she said, as if that explained everything.

Unfortunately, John was still lost. "Yeah, since we were kids. It's the only thing I could think of that rhymed with *Amanda,*" he added, hoping to coax a smile from her.

Pulling her chin free from his grasp, she sighed. "I know."

Hard as he tried, he just couldn't follow her logic. "I don't get it. You're gonna have to draw me a map or something."

After moving away a few steps, she spun and nailed him with a glare. "Every other girl, you call *darlin'.* Even that airhead Ginger, for goodness sake."

Feeling a little airheaded himself, John strained to connect the dots. Then it hit him, and he reached out for her hand. When she scowled and yanked it away, he almost let it go. Something stopped him, though, and he took both her hands in his to draw her closer.

Smiling down at her, he asked, "Didn't you ever wonder *why* I call you something different?"

"I'm just your friend." The answer came quickly, proving that she'd thought about it more than once. "They're the ones chasing after you."

"Sorta." Accustomed to doing things rather than talking about them, he searched for the proper words. Something told him it was crucial that he say this right. "There've been lots of girls, but only one Panda."

She tilted her head in disbelief. "Are you serious?"

"Yes, ma'am."

She wanted to believe him, he could tell. But her disastrous last relationship was making it hard for her to trust him.

Finally, her expression softened, and she gave him a warm, grateful smile. "I'm your Panda."

"Yup. The only one."

Before he knew what was happening, John caught himself tracing the soft curve of her cheek with his finger. Horrified, he pulled back and tapped her cute little nose. To cover his sudden panic, he picked up a dish towel and started in on the pans in the drainer. The quick move put a good arm's length of distance between them, but suddenly that wasn't enough.

The breeze coming through the window picked up the scent of her perfume, a sweet blend of vanilla and something fruity. While they washed and dried, she chattered on about how she'd conquered the washing machine and was brushing up on her American history so she could help Kyle with his upcoming test on the Revolutionary War.

The whole time, John was trying desperately to focus on something other than how dangerously close he'd come to kissing her. Again.

Chapter Five

Around six that evening, Tucker started his usual "someone's here" routine. John glanced up from setting the table to see Matt's huge blue pickup pull into the turnaround. When Amanda groaned, John looked over his shoulder at her. "What?"

"They're early. Supper is at six-thirty."

"So?"

"So I'm not ready," she snapped. "I've got nothing to feed these people."

"*These* people?" he repeated with a chuckle. "It's just Matt and Caty. Y'know, family for our family supper. She probably wanted to get here ahead of time to give you a hand."

Fury blazed in her eyes, and she snarled, "I'm perfectly capable of having supper ready for everyone. At six-thirty."

He'd had just about enough of the uptight attitude that had followed her home from the West

Coast. It was time to put a stop to it. "Oh, lighten up. It's not a big deal."

"This is my job, John," she informed him primly. "If this meal doesn't go well, it'll be my fault."

Since she was obviously set on making a simple meal into a problem, he decided to switch tactics. "Well, everything smells great, and nothing's on fire. How bad could it be?"

She wanted to yell at him—he could see it on her face. So he did what he always did when faced with a woman determined to work herself into a frenzy over nothing. He gave her his biggest, brightest grin.

"Don't you try that on me, Sawyer," she scolded, shaking a scary-looking metal spoon at him. "It won't work."

Despite her words, he got a faint smile for his efforts. Since she'd been coiled like a spring thirty seconds ago, he considered it a success.

"Amanda!" With Hailey cradled in one arm, Caty reached out to hug her. "It's so great to see you. How have you been?"

"Fine." Amanda wiggled the baby's foot and smiled up at Matt. "I see you've been busy."

"Never a dull moment," he replied. "How're things going here?"

"The same. Lisa and Seth aren't here yet, so help yourselves to whatever looks good."

"That'd be everything," John said, winking at her as he snatched a fresh tomato from the chopping block.

When she thanked him, her grateful smile told him she needed the compliment more than he'd realized.

Hailey was fascinated with their visitor, and kept her curious eyes fixed on Amanda while Caty chatted with this newcomer. After a few minutes, Caty asked, "Would you like to hold her?"

Amanda gave the baby a hesitant look. "Are you sure? I mean, I'm a stranger. She might not like me."

"Oh, she loves people."

Amanda took her awkwardly, as if she was afraid to damage the very sturdy little girl. Tucker wasn't nearly as shy. He sniffed Hailey's bare toes, and she yanked her foot away, squealing with laughter. When she put her foot down and reached out for him, Amanda hunkered down to let her pet the dog. He licked her tiny hand, making her laugh again.

Occupied by the outgoing Lab and giggling child, Amanda visibly relaxed. Cuddling Hailey closer, her expression softened into something John had never seen from her. Before he could figure out what it meant, Marianne, Ridge and the kids came into the kitchen.

Matt greeted Ridge with a grin. "Hey there, Pops. What'd the doctor say?"

"Everything's fine," he replied with obvious relief. "We see him every week from now on, though, to be safe."

Suddenly serious, Matt rested a hand on his old buddy's shoulder. "Just let John and me know when you need a break. We'll work it out."

John nodded wholehearted agreement. For the Sawyers, family came first. Period, end of story. "Yeah. No problem."

Ridge gave them each a grateful look. "Thanks."

"Speaking of breaks," Amanda said quietly. "I was hoping to get some time off tomorrow morning. I have some things to take care of. Personal things," she added as if she expected them to challenge her right to a few hours off.

"That works out fine. You can even use the van if you want," Marianne told her. "Kyle has baseball, but his game isn't 'til the afternoon."

"Speaking of tomorrow," Caty chimed in. "Hailey and I were thinking we'd come out for breakfast with everyone before the guys get to work. Is that okay?"

"You mean, to keep an eye on me while the boys are baling and Amanda's gone?" Marianne asked, slanting a look at her husband.

"Of course not." Caty smiled over at her daughter. "We love being at the farm, don't we, june bug?"

Hailey gurgled a reply, which made everyone laugh. While they finalized the details for coming and going, John watched Amanda closely. She struck him as someone who'd never held a baby in her life, but Hailey could soften a heart made of stone. Gradually, Amanda relaxed and actually seemed to be enjoying her time with the newest Sawyer.

When the arrangements were settled, Marianne added, "Amanda, we saw Pastor Charles in town this afternoon. He wanted us to tell you he's glad you're home and he'd love to have you in church on Sunday."

"That's sweet, but church isn't really my kind of thing. I've had a busy week, so it would be nice to sleep in on Sunday."

That didn't sit well with Marianne, who pressed her lips into a disapproving line. She'd never insist that their housekeeper go to church, but she definitely would have preferred it. John wasn't crazy about it, either, but he kept his mouth shut. He'd already suspected Amanda had turned away from her Christian upbringing, and this confirmed it for him. She had a lot to deal with, and leaning on God would make it easier to manage. But he'd learned that however hard you might try, you couldn't convince people how important faith was. You had to show them.

Even then, it only worked if they were open to God in the first place. Nothing ever got into a closed mind, Ethan used to tell him. Frustrating as it was for him to watch her struggle, John knew there was nothing to do but be patient and wait for her to come around.

And if she never did, that was her choice.

Hailey glanced at John, her face lighting up as if she'd just noticed him. With a delighted squeal, she reached both hands up, eyes dancing with very flattering baby approval.

"She really likes you," Amanda commented, sounding more than a little impressed.

"Sometimes I think she likes John better than me," Matt grumbled with a wry grin.

As if on cue, the oven timer went off. Standing, Amanda handed off the squirming child to him. Obviously rattled for some reason, she seemed relieved to escape to the other side of the kitchen. He still wasn't sure what was bugging her, but John decided to create a little diversion to give her a chance to get comfortable again.

"Is that right, little darlin'?" he asked, rubbing noses with his niece. When she babbled back at him, he listened carefully before looking over at Matt. "Don't feel too bad, big brother. She's not the first girl who liked me better than you."

"Right. Name one."

"Jeannie Randall. Karen Masterson." Grinning wider, he went in for the kill. "Caty Lee McKenzie."

"Oh, please!" She laughed. "That was such a long time ago."

"But she liked me better," he assured Hailey. "Don't you let your daddy tell you any different."

"Keep it up, Goldilocks," Matt growled. "You'll be baling that hayfield all by yourself this weekend."

John grinned but decided to be smart and ease up on his big brother. Thanks to Caty, Matt was a lot less intense than he used to be, but the old grizzly bear still reared up every once in a while. It was best not to rile him too much.

"Can't have that," Ridge said as the kids settled onto the bench at the table. "Seeing as your birthday's coming up, you should start taking it easier."

Hailey giggled, and John gave her a mock frown. "What's so funny?"

Eyes shining with good humor, she babbled a response, punctuating it with another giggle. "Yeah, well, when it's your birthday, I'm gonna laugh at you."

"John," Lisa scolded from the door, "don't you dare pick on my sweet baby niece."

Shouting excitedly, Kyle and Emily ran to greet

the newlyweds, wrapping them in hugs while the adults hovered behind, waiting for their turn.

"Did you bring us anything?" Emily asked, eyes shining hopefully.

Her mother chided her, but Seth grinned as he hefted two large bags. "Did you really think we'd forget?"

"Later, though," Lisa told her as they sat down at the table. "Supper smells great, and we're starving."

She added a smile for Amanda, who returned it as she set a huge platter of corn bread in the middle of the table. "Welcome home, you two. How was Europe?"

"Amazing, of course," Lisa replied, grasping Seth's left hand. His simple gold band still looked odd there, and John wondered how long it took a guy to get used to wearing one. "Amanda Gardner, this is my husband, Seth Hansen."

"I've heard a lot of great things about you," Amanda told him as she finally sat down.

"All true," Lisa assured her, hugging his arm.

They heard all about the honeymoon while they worked their way through Amanda's delicious meal. Other domestic chores might be a challenge for her, but she had nothing to worry about in the cooking department, John thought with a grin. Everything was great.

During a lull in the conversation, Marianne

asked, "Can everyone make it out here for supper on Tuesday?"

They all chimed in with yeses, and John folded his arms with a scowl. "I'm busy."

"No, you're not." She wagged a scolding finger at him. "Thirty was last year and we let you be. Not this time."

"Whatever."

"That's not a very good attitude, Uncle John," Emily informed him sternly. "It's your special day, and we want to make a cake and have presents for you. It'll be fun—you'll see."

She was so earnest, he had to grin. "When you put it like that, it sounds great. I'll be there."

"Six o'clock." Pushing a straw into her berry drink box, she fixed him with a very serious look. "Please be on time."

Folding his arms on the table, John chuckled. "You sound like your mom."

"You're late all the time," Kyle reminded him. "The party's really at six-thirty."

"Kyle," Marianne chided in a whisper. "You weren't supposed to tell him that."

"We're guys, Mom. We have to stick together."

"Thanks, buddy. I appreciate it." John fist-bumped Kyle across the table, which was rude but funny.

While the family laughed over the whole thing, Marianne caught John's gaze and held it for a few moments. She knew why he didn't like celebrating his birthday anymore, and it had nothing to do with turning thirty, thirty-one or even eighty. He hated that she was pushing him to do it, but the kids were so excited, he didn't have the heart to disappoint them.

Lisa briefly rubbed his shoulder before heading back for more food. Unfortunately, Amanda saw the odd exchange, and she gave John a baffled look before opening the oven to take out the first batch of spare ribs. Hoping he appeared convincing, he shrugged as if he had no clue what had motivated Lisa's affectionate gesture.

But he knew perfectly well, and being reminded that his birthday was just around the corner dimmed his usual enjoyment of their weekly supper. A Sawyer family tradition, it wasn't easy to get everyone here these days. But they all made time for it because it was important to sit down and reconnect with each other.

The hand-hewn oak table had stood in the same spot since the 1850s, when Daniel Sawyer carved it for his wife's new kitchen. Sitting around it, trading stories and jokes over a good meal, was something the current Sawyers had done for as long as any of them could remember. Adding kids to the mix made it more lively, and during their busiest season, it was a great way to unwind.

John wasn't sure if it was by design or not, but

by the time Amanda was ready to sit down, the only open seat was next to him. A quick glance around the crowd showed him a bunch of innocent feminine looks, which pretty much answered his question.

Somehow, Marianne and Lisa had arranged the seating so Amanda would be forced to sit beside John. They hadn't had even thirty seconds alone to set this up, which told him they'd conferred earlier and decided to take a shot at matchmaking.

Poor girls, he thought as he forked a pair of ribs off the platter. They didn't realize that he and Amanda had never seen—and would never see—anything even remotely romantic in each other. They were such different people, being friends was tough enough. Making a relationship work would be impossible.

His nosy sisters and sister-in-law were going to be mighty disappointed when their efforts led to absolutely nothing.

Amanda's first Sawyer family supper was a rousing success.

Everyone enjoyed her spare ribs and corn bread, and Matt even tossed in a compliment about her sweet tea.

"That's good to hear. I haven't made it in so long, I thought for sure I'd forgotten how."

"It's wonderful to see you again." Lisa reached

over to hug her around the shoulders. "How does it feel to be back?"

"Well, I've been pretty busy, but things are fine so far." Amanda slanted a look at John, who just grinned back. True to his word as ever, he'd done nothing to clue the family in about her predicament. "I wish I could have been here for your wedding. Do you have pictures?"

A multi-stage groan rippled around the table, and they all made some kind of disparaging princess comment. Except for Emily, who piped up, "I'd love to see them again, Aunt Lisa. Do you have your phone?"

Lisa smiled. "We'll look at them later, sweetness. I think everyone else might like to see our new photos from Europe."

That idea went over much better, and they all jammed together so they had a view of the small screen.

"This is us at the Coliseum in Rome." Turning the phone, she swiped her finger across the screen to go through the shots. "We waited all morning to get in, but it was worth it."

"Seems to me you went all that way for nothing," John commented to her husband, Seth, who was as reserved as Lisa was bubbly. "We got lots of old, falling-down buildings around here."

Seth grinned but wouldn't take the bait and annoy his new wife. Smart man.

"This one." Lisa waved the phone for emphasis, "was finished in the year 80 and is mostly still standing. Our country is a baby compared to all the places we visited over there."

"How come all those stones are missing?" Kyle asked.

"Earthquakes took out that big chunk on the side. During the Middle Ages they weren't using it, so they stripped off pieces to use in other buildings." She frowned at the picture. "It must have been amazing when it was covered in white marble."

While she continued her honeymoon show-and-tell, Amanda couldn't help feeling a little envious. She'd been to all those places herself, but she hadn't gotten half the enjoyment out of them that Lisa and Seth obviously had. Then again, she'd been with a tour group, not sharing the sights with a man who loved her so much he felt compelled to marry her.

Lisa had really done well. So had Marianne and Caty, for that matter. Amanda had yet to find the man she trusted enough to give him carte blanche in her life. Sometimes, like now, she wondered if he even existed.

Chapter Six

Something wasn't right.

Amanda lay in her bed, still foggy from the best night's sleep she'd had in months. While her fuzzy brain tried to figure out what was wrong, the plaid curtains shifted in a breeze scented with honeysuckle. When she was able to pick up four distinct versions of birdsong, it finally hit her what was wrong.

The house was silent.

Normally filled with boisterous Sawyers and farmhands, the large farmhouse was so quiet she could hear the fridge humming away down in the kitchen. It was a lazy, luxurious feeling, as if the house itself was resting, waiting for everyone to come back and fill it up again.

Smiling at the foolish turn her imagination had taken, she plumped up her pillow and leaned back to enjoy the solitude. Even after spending years at the breakneck pace of the advertising and PR business, she'd never had a busier week in her life. Getting accustomed to the time change had been more challenging than she'd anticipated, not to mention becoming acquainted with the new people who called the farm *home*.

Hailey was a peach—every inch her mother's child. Ridge and the kids were great, and the newlywed Hansens were absolutely adorable together. After a while, she'd even managed to draw Seth into a spirited conversation about Baroque Italian architecture.

Her biggest challenge was John. No surprise there, she decided with a sigh. While she was mulling that over, a squirrel appeared outside her window, blinking in at her with curiosity.

"Hello there," she said quietly. Even that was too much for him, though, and he disappeared into the misty morning.

Looking at the clock, she saw it was almost ten. She used to sleep well into the afternoon, but those days were over. After church, the Sawyers were having lunch before the guys headed out for an afternoon in the fields. Outside her window, she could see acre upon acre of hay and oats, rippling in the breeze like waves.

It looked endless to her. She could only imagine how large the farm looked when you went over it a foot at a time. Day after day, year after year, she mused with a frown. With over two thousand acres, they finished one section just in time to start on another. And then they replanted and started the whole cycle over again.

How did John stand it? With her very short attention span, she'd go completely bonkers within a week. Not everyone was meant to be a farmer, she reasoned as she stretched and reluctantly got out of bed. Now that she'd gotten an up-close view of what it took to run a farm this size, she really admired the Sawyers for maintaining their family business. She was certain that, at one time or another, they'd been offered a lot of money for this place.

After showering, she pulled on a pair of workout shorts and a faded tie-dyed T-shirt she used to wear only for yoga class. Recalling John's compliment about her more natural appearance, she checked the mirror. Tilting her head one way and then another, spinning around to see her back, she had no clue what he liked so much.

She really needed some clothes, she thought with disdain. Maybe during the week she could get out and do a little shopping at the discount strip mall she'd noticed while running errands in Kenwood yesterday. Very little shopping, she amended with a frown. She couldn't keep using the Collinses' minivan—she needed money to fix her car. Probably lots of money.

Since she had time, she debated drying her hair or just pulling it up into a ponytail the way she'd been doing. Realizing it didn't matter to her current employers, she went with the ponytail because it was easier. Having spent years focused on every detail of her appearance, it was liberating not to care anymore.

Her solid night's sleep had left her with a little more bounce, and she trotted downstairs to find Tucker lying in front of the screen door in the kitchen, gazing longingly out at the day. When he saw her, he thumped his tail halfheartedly on the floor, his brow furrowed in a woe-is-me kind of expression.

"Poor baby." She crouched down to pet him. "Wanna go out?"

He was like a brand-new dog. Jumping to his feet, he wrapped his paws around her waist, looking from her to the door as if he couldn't wait to get going. Laughing, she opened the screen for him and went to the cereal cupboard for something to eat. When she heard whining, she found him framed in the doorway, looking pathetic.

"You want company, too?" He yipped, spinning before coming to a stop, tongue wagging hopefully.

"Okay, hang on."

She traded the cereal box for a banana and joined the irresistible Lab on the porch. Delighted, he took off down the lane that wound past John's house, disturbing a cluster of blue jays that scolded him as he raced past. Amanda followed at a more leisurely pace, enjoying the clean feeling of the air as the mist evaporated with the rising sun.

She remembered playing in the old carriage house with the Sawyers when they were kids, climbing into the loft, daring each other to do gymnastics routines on the rough-hewn beams. Stupid, she recalled with a fond smile. It was amazing that they hadn't broken their necks. Built to complement the main house, the cottage couldn't look any more different if someone tried.

The lines of the cream-colored building were well-proportioned, she decided, and the porch was a nice touch. But it was empty. Unlike the family's home, where you could see Marianne's touch everywhere. She had flowers and plants twining in and around the gardens and the porches, while porch swings and comfy chairs beckoned people to come up and sit awhile.

John's place looked blank by comparison. As if he spent all his time elsewhere and only crashed there at night. Which was pretty much how it was, she realized as she considered the small house. It was easy to envision some wicker chairs on the porch, baskets of bright flowers hanging between the porch posts. Then there was that space out back, overlooking the pond. With a little work and a nice grill, it would be a great spot for him to relax in.

Maybe, if it was nicer, he could even host some of their gatherings there. It might make a pleasant change of scenery for everyone.

Then again, it wasn't her place to suggest something like that. She'd seen his reaction when she mentioned redecorating. Not panic, exactly, but not thrilled, either. He had his little bachelor pad, with its huge bed and TV and cobwebs under the kitchen chairs. It baffled her why anyone would want to live that way, but apparently he did.

She just couldn't understand why.

John pulled his car into its usual spot in the turnaround and headed for the house. It was nearly eleven, and he figured even a city girl like Amanda would be up by now. He was still bothered by whatever she was keeping from the family, and he'd driven home like a maniac to get some time alone with her before everyone else showed up. One way or another, she was going to tell him what was going on.

When he noticed her staring at his house, all thoughts of confronting her flew straight out of his head. He hurried down the lane to put his foot down before it was too late. "Whatever you're thinking, forget about it."

Turning, she gave him the prettiest blank look he'd ever seen. "What?"

"I know that look. You're redecorating my place."

"I have a few ideas—"

"It's fine the way it is," he insisted. "Leave it be."

"What about the back? A patio's not hard to put in, and you'd have a great view of the pond all summer."

She was trying to be nice, so John tamped down his frustration and spoke calmly. "By the time I could sit down and look at it, it'd be dark."

"You'd see the moon," she argued. "Hanging over the trees, reflected in the water. It's so pretty."

Narrowing his eyes, he asked, "How do you know?"

"I remember." Looking in that direction, she added a nostalgic smile. "Sitting out on the dock with our feet in the water, looking up at the stars. It's one of the reasons I wanted to come back. I was hoping it would still feel the same way."

The sentimental confession spoke volumes about how lost she'd been feeling, and he stepped up behind her. Putting his hands on her shoulders, he wished he could fight off whatever seemed to be haunting her. "It does, I promise."

Leaning back against him, she asked, "You still do that?"

"Sometimes. It's not the same without you, though."

Wincing, John wished he could snatch those words back. What had possessed him to say them? She was going to think he'd been pining for her all these years, when in fact he'd done just the opposite. Sure, he thought about her once in a while, wondering what she was up to. But that was the full extent of it.

It wasn't as if he'd missed her. At least, not until she'd reappeared in Harland with her fancy life collapsing around her. The past few days, he'd been forced to admit that, despite the years that had passed, Amanda Gardner was still very much under his skin.

Being friends with her had been easy enough when they were kids. Now, there was a bizarre new twist to that relationship, and he hadn't quite nailed it down yet. Judging by the look on her face when she turned to him, she didn't get it, either.

"You missed me?" she asked in a disbelieving tone.

Stunned by her reaction, it took John a few moments to realize that she'd spun on a dime and was neatly circled in his arms. It would be so easy to reel her in for an actual hug. Or even something more.

Fighting off that impulse was almost impossible.

Being this close to her was dangerous, but he didn't want her to think he was pulling away from her. Keeping his hold loose and friendly, he gave her what he hoped came across as a casual grin. "Sure, but not in a bad way. I just wondered how you were, what you were doing."

Who you were doing it with.

Disgusted by the turn his mind had taken, he swallowed a groan. It seemed a part of him considered Amanda more than just a buddy who looked cute in a pleated skirt and pom-poms. When that had happened, he had no idea, but he wasn't happy about it.

His nice, simple life had suddenly gotten very complicated. And with Amanda settled at the farm until the babies were born, it wasn't likely to get any easier.

John hated his birthday.

It wasn't the day so much, he amended while he pulled on his good boots Tuesday evening. It was the celebrating part. But it was important to his family, and, as Marianne had pointed out, they'd let his thirtieth slip by quietly. The kids had been whispering to each other about some surprise or another, stopping when they saw him coming.

So, because it meant so much to them, he'd put on a smile and pretend to enjoy himself. Pausing by his front door, he glanced at the shelf that held the conference MVP award from his senior year of football. The gleaming silver had a mirror effect, and in a flat section he saw a perfect reflection of himself.

Sad, he decided with a sigh. Even when he pulled out a grin, his eyes still held the sorrow of a day he was beginning to think he'd never be able to celebrate again. Pushing the morose thought down, he focused on why he was going along with this party. The kids, his family—they all needed to believe he was okay with it.

He caught himself dragging his feet on the way up the path and conjured a memory of his old football coach to give him a little pep talk.

Challenges are part of life, son. It's how you handle 'em that makes you who you are.

Buoyed by those inspiring words, he entered the kitchen to a chorus of birthday wishes, backslapping and warm hugs. They'd banished him from the kitchen after lunch, and now he understood why. Streamers hung everywhere, with helium balloons of every color tied wherever there was space.

"This looks awesome, guys," he said, leaning down to hug Marianne and Lisa. "Thanks."

"Oh, this was Amanda and the kids," Marianne informed him. "I had an online final exam today, and Lisa was busy with Seth."

"Kyle and Emily made all the decorations," Amanda clarified. "I worked the helium tank, but they were like a couple of birthday beavers."

She ruffled Emily's hair, but held up her hand for a high-five from Kyle. Apparently, she'd picked up on his newfound hatred of anything he deemed remotely childish. John was impressed with how quickly she'd acclimated to running someone else's household. Having been the boss in her old job, she'd settled into her new role nicely.

That's how she'd be with her own children someday, he realized. Warm and encouraging, understanding that every kid was different and needed a special touch.

Alarmed by the direction his thoughts had wandered in, he yanked himself back to the table filled with people. When Matt shifted to offer him a seat, John grinned. "Forty's just around the corner for you, big brother."

"Say that again, and you won't see thirty-two."

Later that evening, after everyone had gone home and settled in for the night, Amanda looked out the kitchen window toward John's house. Completely dark, it looked lonely for company. Since the guys were done working for the day, she thought maybe John had a date he hadn't mentioned. A quick glance outside showed his car still parked beside the equipment barn.

Where had he gotten to? she wondered as she dried her hands on a dish towel. She was no psychiatrist, but anyone with two eyes and half a brain could figure out he wasn't a hundred percent into his birthday party. Recalling how he'd tried to discourage them from doing anything at all, she frowned. The John she grew up with loved attention of any kind. For him to avoid it seemed very out of character.

Just as she was about to turn away, she caught a flash of movement near the old oak that stood at the top of a small hill not far from the house. Her intuition told her she'd found the birthday boy, and she grabbed the dessert plate holding his untouched piece of cake and a fork. Carrying it outside, she headed for the tree. She found him sitting on the ground, eyes closed, his head tipped back against the gnarled trunk.

Tears streaming down his face.

He hadn't heard her coming, and she suddenly realized this was a bad idea. Despite her good intentions, he obviously wanted to be alone with whatever was troubling him. Feeling like an intruder, she quietly backed away, but her feet rustled in the grass.

His eyes popped open, and he looked her way with a guilty expression. Wiping his cheeks with his palms, he sighed into his open hands before meeting her eyes. "Hey."

"Hey yourself." Feeling incredibly awkward, she held out the plate. "You didn't have any cake."

"Thanks. Maybe later."

The tremor in his voice rattled her so thoroughly, she didn't know what to do. Men usually wanted solitude when they were upset, so they could do whatever it was they did to get through it. But she couldn't just leave him sitting here, looking so miserable it made her heart ache.

Instead, she decided to take a chance and sat down beside him. "Wanna tell me?"

"Not really."

"Okay. Do you want me to leave you alone?"

That got her a wry grin. "Not really."

Progress, she thought with a measure of pride. Since she'd been at the farm, they'd both gone out of their way to keep things light and friendly. The line wasn't firm, but neither of them had crossed over it. Much as she wanted to help him, Amanda figured the best approach was to let him come to her. He was used to women chasing him, she reasoned, but he didn't confide in them. Maybe the opposite strategy would work.

After a few minutes of silence, he picked up a hunk of dried-up bark and began crumbling it into pieces. Without looking up, he said, "You want to know why I hate my birthday, right?"

"Only if you want to tell me."

Tossing the bark away, he fixed her with the most mournful expression she'd ever seen in her life. "It's Dad's birthday, too."

Of course. Cursing her atrocious memory, Amanda gave herself a mental head slap. John and Ethan had always shared that day, with tons of food and a humongous cake for the hundred or so people who showed up to celebrate with them. The Sawyers did everything big, and Amanda had often thought the festivities resembled a wedding more than a birthday party.

"That's why Marianne made such a big deal out of this," Amanda said. "She thinks it will help you get past Ethan's death."

"It won't work. Nothing ever will, because it's my fault he's gone."

"No." She heard the agony in his voice, and knew it was misplaced. Taking one of his strong hands in both of hers, she said, "Caty told me it was a heart attack. That's not anyone's fault."

"It was so hot that day. We were bringing in the last cutting of hay, pushing to beat the rain that was coming in. I tried to talk him into letting me finish up, but he wouldn't." Pausing, John swallowed so hard she could almost feel it. "We got the wagon to the barn, and he grabbed his chest. He couldn't breathe, and I caught him right before he fell. I called 911, but it was too late. He smiled up at me, and then he was gone."

The fresh tears on his cheeks were almost the end of her. Amanda remembered Ethan Sawyer, a warm, compassionate widower who'd single-handedly raised four young children. Never too busy for a chat, he'd been a welcome harbor when her own parents were too consumed with other things to notice that she needed them.

But giving in to her belated grief wouldn't help John. He needed sympathy, not a blubbering woman to comfort. So she swallowed her emotions and held his hand, wishing there was something she could do.

"Matt kind of gets it," John confided in a strangled whisper. "He felt guilty about not being here to help, and it took him a long time to get over it. But I *was* here, and I could see Dad was tired. should've convinced him to stop."

"No one ever convinced Ethan of anything," Amanda reminded him gently. "You know that as well as anyone. He was a wonderful man, but rock-stubborn right down to his boots. Just like you."

John glanced up, and she gave him her brightest smile. "I've always admired that about you. Both of you," she added to keep Ethan in the conversation.

Since even his own family couldn't convince John he wasn't responsible for his father's death, she knew arguing that angle was a lost cause. Maybe if she got him to focus on positive memories, he could begin to let go of the guilt he'd been carrying around.

"Thanks." Giving her a faint smile, he cocked his head and looked through the branches at the moon overhead. "Y'know, at first I couldn't get through a day without feeling like I was gonna lose it. Matt was home, and he tried to help, but he didn't know what to do anymore than I did. I still think about Dad all the time, especially today." He closed his eyes, and his shoulders lifted in a heavy sigh. "If I could skip today every year, I would."

He didn't say anything more, but she sensed he wasn't ready to go inside just yet. A warm breeze floated in, and the leaf-laden branches creaked as they swayed overhead. Frogs that lived around the pond chimed in with the night birds, surrounding the farm in a subdued melody that seemed in keeping with John's mood.

Sitting there with him, in the most peaceful place she'd ever known, it was easy to feel nostalgic, and Amanda gladly went along with it. "You know, I remember how you, Matt and your dad used to eat lunch here while you were working. I'd look out and wonder what you were talking about."

John shrugged, but some of the misery left his face. "Farm stuff, mostly. Sometimes Dad would tell us about the first Sawyers on this place, back before Harland even existed. Taking down trees to build a cabin and a barn, then this house later on."

"I always thought it looked like they added onto it over the years."

"Yeah, they did. It's a good thing, too," he added with a chuckle. "Matt and I would've killed each other if we had to share a room."

Considering Matt's temper and John's knack for tweaking it, murder was only a slight exaggeration, and they both laughed. As they sat there reminiscing, Amanda felt herself being drawn back to when things were blissfully uncomplicated, and she believed nothing truly awful would ever happen to her or her best friend John.

If only she'd known just how difficult life could be, she lamented with a sigh. She'd have enjoyed those days more.

Chapter Seven

Memorial Day, John was pensive as he lay in bed and listened to the morning DJ read names from a list of local soldiers who'd given their lives for their country. Most of the recent ones he recognized—men and women he'd known all his life, people he'd gone to school with. The older ones were fathers, grandfathers and uncles of longtime friends.

His immediate family hadn't seen combat since the war between the states, but John had a healthy respect for anyone who served. His brother-in-law, Seth, was still recovering from PTSD, which gave John a newfound admiration for what soldiers went through.

It was a somber start to the day, but the bright sunshine got him up and going. Oddly, since his soul-baring conversation with Amanda several days ago, he'd slept like a rock. Maybe talking about Ethan was a good idea, after all. Only with Amanda, though. He wasn't ready to lay all those raw feelings out in front of anyone else.

As he strolled up the lane toward the house, Tucker loped out to meet him. A brand-new stars-and-stripes bandanna had replaced the ratty old one, and the Lab strutted proudly alongside John as they went up the back steps. Even before he opened the door, he heard trouble. Woman trouble.

"I am *not* using that thing," Marianne was seething. "I'm pregnant, not paralyzed."

Fighting off a grin, John swung open the door. "Good morning to you, too."

Sitting on her usual throne, she turned to him with a peeved expression. "John, explain to this man—" she waved absently in Ridge's direction "—that I do *not* need a wheelchair."

Glancing into the corner, John saw what looked to him like a nice, modern wheelchair. "Whose is that?"

"I borrowed it from Priscilla Fairman." Ridge aimed an amused look at his very stubborn wife. "Who also insisted she didn't need it."

"That's different," Marianne huffed. "Priscilla broke her ankle."

"If I hadn't caught you on the steps at church yesterday," John pointed out, "you'd have broken your ankle, too."

"Ridiculous."

"Hey, it's totally understandable." John plunked himself down on the bench and started digging for the sports section. "If I couldn't see my own feet, I'd be tripping, too."

He didn't look up, but he could feel his big sister trying to laser a hole in his skull. Fury poured off her in waves, and he knew her arms were folded over top of the twins. Sawyer girls were like that, he knew from vast personal experience. His sisters, and all his female relatives were spitfires, every one of them. Amanda fit the mold perfectly.

Where had that come from? After a brief jolt of panic, he decided it was just early and he wasn't completely awake yet.

Taking the seat beside John, Ridge got uncharacteristically serious with Marianne. Which told John just how much worry his brother-in-law was carting around these days. "You're not walking anywhere outside this house anymore. End of discussion."

"I don't want everyone seeing me in that."

"The football team's heading up the parade this year, Mom," Kyle reminded her through a mouthful of cereal.

"Don't talk with your mouth full," she snapped. Obediently, he swallowed. "You're the team mom. Don't you want to see all us Wildcats in our gear, walking down Main Street with our trophy?"

"Of course I do."

"Nancy's bringing her new ducklings, Mommy," Emily chimed in. "There's a lot of them, and she needs me to help pull her wagon."

"Ridge, you can take the kids," Amanda offered while she flipped pancakes on the griddle. "I'll stay here with Marianne."

"Not a chance," John protested. Amanda had always been a social butterfly, and her reluctance to leave the farm baffled—and worried—him. "You haven't been into town once since you got back. Folks are gonna start to wonder if you've grown an extra head or something."

She opened her mouth, probably to fire off some of that sharp wit she loved to fling around. Apparently, she thought better of it and just stuck her tongue out at him. Not exactly polite, but he was making progress with her. She'd gotten to be less careful around him, which was a huge improvement over where they'd stood just last week.

Leaning back, Ridge stared silently at his wife. Even though he didn't speak, his demeanor clearly said he wasn't budging.

Outmaneuvered, Marianne finally relented with a warm smile for Kyle. "I wouldn't miss it."

"We'd better get a move on, then," Amanda said. "The kids have to be there early to get lined up."

She set a platter of steaming pancakes in the middle of the table and sat down with a bowl of plain oatmeal. No brown sugar, no syrup. Just oatmeal. Weird.

"I've never marched before, Amanda," Emily confided with a slight frown. "Have you?"

Amanda gave her a bright smile. "All the time. Your uncle John and I marched with the football team and cheerleaders every year in high school."

"With the trophy," he added proudly. "They're still in the case at Harland High."

"Those were the days, huh?" Ridge teased.

"Fun times," he agreed, grinning across the table at Amanda. "Amanda was cheer captain all four years."

Emily's eyes widened in awe. "You must've been really good."

"Mostly, I was the only one brave enough to get tossed in the air and be on top of our formations."

"Don't let her fool you, sweetness," John said. "She was awesome."

Grinning, Amanda dug into her bland breakfast. He couldn't fathom why she'd want to eat that when there were plenty of buttermilk pancakes and bacon to go around. That was probably how she'd gotten to be the size of a fence rail. He'd work on her today, though. The town picnic would be full of irresistible, fattening things to eat. If he really put his mind to it, he had no doubt he could get her to loosen up and indulge a little.

John rarely got a day off this time of year, and knowing he'd be spending this one with Amanda made it feel extraspecial. He hadn't looked forward to a parade this much in a long time.

Amanda couldn't remember the last time she'd actually celebrated Memorial Day. Taking advantage of the holiday, she'd go into the office and get more accomplished than she usually did in a week. With no interruptions or distractions, no ringing phones, texts or email alerts, it was one of the most productive days she had all year long.

This one would be productive, too, she supposed. Just in a different way. While she packed fried chicken and various salads into Marianne's picnic hamper, she found herself smiling. The thing was enormous, and she hated to imagine the size of the meal that would actually fill it.

She carefully laid the pies on top—cherry, blueberry and apple—and wasn't surprised when the lid closed with room to spare. When she tried to lift it, she got a rude shock. It weighed about half a ton, and she wasn't sure she could move it gracefully enough to keep everything inside from toppling over.

"Don't worry." Coming up behind her, John stepped in without being asked. "I got it."

She elbowed him out of the way and grasped the handles firmly. "I can do it."

Without blinking, he moved back, hands raised in surrender. He didn't say anything, just leaned down to lift the full ice chest from the floor.

She appreciated his letting her manage on her own. Because of her small stature, most guys assumed she was helpless. "Thank you."

"For letting you be stubborn or for helping with the cooler?" he asked with a knowing grin.

"Both."

Once she got the basket balanced, she led the way to the back door. She pushed it open and held it for John, then followed him out to the Collinses' van.

After they got everything loaded, John turned to her with another grin. "I'm glad you're coming with us. It'll be fun."

Amanda wished she could share his confidence. "I hope so."

His grin mellowed into something softer, and his gaze warmed as he brushed a stray curl out of her eyes. "It will, Panda. You'll see."

"I haven't seen these people in forever. Most of them probably won't even remember me."

"Are you kidding? Local girl in the Hollywood spotlight? Folks still ask me how you're doing out there, when you're coming back. Now you can tell 'em yourself."

Something in his tone told her those conversations weren't always pleasant for him. She could only guess how difficult it was to continue fielding questions about an old friend who'd basically turned her back on him years ago. But he'd told her very plainly to quit apologizing for that, so she settled for what she hoped was a bright smile. "Sounds good."

Ridge appeared behind them and slid the offending wheelchair into an open spot. "We'd better get going before Marianne changes her mind again."

John chuckled in sympathy. "Pregnancy sure does a number on a woman's personality, doesn't it?"

"Tell me about it." Rubbing his neck with his hand, Ridge gave John a hopeful look. "It'll get better, right?"

"Sure, in a couple months. Once the twins are here, you'll be so tired you won't notice Marianne's mood swings anymore."

"Thanks a lot."

Once everyone was settled in the three rows of the van, they headed for town. Fortunately, the marchers had to be there early, because half an hour later there wasn't a parking spot to be had anywhere within a mile of the parade route.

Amanda suspected Ridge had spread the word about Marianne's condition, because not one single person mentioned the wheelchair. The fact that they'd all go along with his request was so touching, it made Amanda a little misty. She'd spent so many years away, she'd forgotten how caring the people of Harland were.

She felt awkward at first, wondering how folks would react when they saw her again after all these years. Before long, she discovered that John was right. Every one of them remembered her, stopping to ask how she liked being home again. After she'd spent thirteen years away, they still considered Harland her home. To her surprise, Amanda realized that she did, too.

That must be why, of all the places she'd passed during her long trip across the country, she'd never questioned where she was heading. Maybe, somewhere deep in her heart, she knew this tiny Carolina town was where she needed to be.

All along Main Street, flags waved from every house, building and lamppost. Bunting swagged along the railings, and "Thank you, veterans" signs were posted wherever there was space. It was like watching an old movie, set in a time when traditional values still meant something.

Why had she ever wanted to forget this? Amanda searched her memory but couldn't come up with the answer. When she was younger, Harland had felt so small, its laid-back pace much too slow for her. Now, rather than a place trapped in the past, it seemed like a beacon of hope and solidity in a world that spun way too fast for her to keep up.

The mushy perspective caught her by surprise, because she wasn't one to think about things that way. The sentimental theme of the day must be getting to her.

At the end of the route, a small military band appeared, and its conductor raised his pristine white gloves. The drummer started the familiar rim beats to keep them in step as they began marching. Walking backwards, the director led them down the street and stopped next to the square. As if on cue, everyone in the crowd stood and removed their caps for the opening chords of "The Star Spangled Banner." With hands over their hearts, they sang along in a variety of voices that amused Amanda even as she sang with them.

This was home, she thought with a smile. This was why she'd come back.

After the somber opening, the parade swung into celebration mode. The champion Wildcats and their enthusiastic cheer squad led the way, and Amanda cheered when she saw Kyle right up front with the other team captains. Local volunteer firefighters and EMTs drove their gleaming trucks through town, blaring their horns and sirens while their kids threw candy out to the crowd.

Emily and her friend were laughing while they

pulled a wagon filled with ducklings up the parade route. Other kids had their 4-H project goats and chickens, and several pretty horses high-stepped along with the music from the band. Amanda was busily snapping pictures with her phone when she noticed something that made her blink and look again.

A boy who looked about ten was guiding a huge hog with a fluffy pink ribbon along the street. Grinning ear to ear, he waved to Amanda as she snapped his picture. That was something you just didn't see every day.

After the parade, everyone assembled in the square for a short ceremony. Shaded by huge trees and surrounded on four sides by churches, in the center stood a monument to all the Harland soldiers who had lost their lives in combat. Each of the clergymen made a brief statement, picking up where the one before had left off. When Pastor Charles stood to end the speeches, Amanda paid special attention. This was the man who'd graciously invited her to his church. Even though she'd declined the invitation, his kind gesture had touched her very much.

"I don't have much to add," he began with a nod toward his fellow clergy. Turning back, he skimmed the crowd with keen eyes. When that fatherly gaze landed on her, Amanda realized he'd been looking for her, and she smiled.

"But this I'm sure of," he continued. "Once a Harlander, always a Harlander. Wherever one of us might go, those we left behind will keep us in their hearts. Always loved, and never forgotten."

Amanda applauded along with everyone else before following the Sawyers to the spot they'd claimed earlier by spreading three large patchwork quilts on the ground. While she knew perfectly well the pastor had been talking about soldiers who'd passed on, she couldn't shake the feeling that he'd intended his message to hold a special meaning for her. Someone who'd left but, judging by her warm reception this morning, was still thought of fondly. It gave her a warm, fuzzy feeling.

Amanda had spent most of the morning preparing and packing their lunch, but the Sawyer crew demolished it in about twenty minutes. Without a schedule to keep, they all pitched in to clean up and lazed around chatting for a while. When the three kids got fidgety, their parents took them over to the playground, and Seth and Lisa wandered over to join some friends nearby.

That left Amanda alone with John, who seemed in no hurry to go. Now that their lively group was gone, she couldn't think of anything to talk about. Staring up at the tree they were sitting under, she asked, "Is this new?"

"Sure is." Leaning back on his elbows, John

glanced up at it, then over to the church. "The old one caved in the church roof last Thanksgiving. Seth headed up the repair crew, and before he left for home he planted this tree because Lisa liked the old one so much."

A detail in the sweet story confused her. "He left? Why?"

John shrugged. "He thought it was time to go, I guess. Christmas Eve he figured out he was in love with Lisa, so he came back. On New Year's Eve, he asked her to marry him."

"Very romantic."

"Yeah, I guess."

She couldn't miss the lack of interest in John's drawl. "Not your style, plowboy?"

"Being married's not my style," he replied with a grimace.

"Well, of course not," she teased. "That would seriously cramp your dating life."

"Got that right."

The lively exchange was fun but over much too quickly. Since he seemed intent on hanging out with her, Amanda hunted for something else to talk about. Her gaze wandered to the little white church she'd attended while she was growing up. Every Sunday, dressed in her nicest clothes, she'd gone to Sunday school and later sung hymns and listened to sermons with the adults. She didn't hate it, by any means, but it hadn't left her with a burning desire to continue the practice.

"It's hard to believe how bad the damage was," she said. "Can you show me how you guys fixed it up?"

He gave her a puzzled look, then shrugged. "Sure."

Standing, he offered her a hand up. She landed much closer to him than she'd meant to and nearly lost her balance. Fortunately, he caught her before she could embarrass herself, and she murmured her thanks.

"I'd never let you fall." Framed by the sparse branches of the young tree, he stood in a spotlight of sunshine. As he grinned down at her, her heart melted just a little, and she barely stifled a sigh.

This man was walking trouble, she reminded herself. He'd sailed through dozens of women, dropping anchor briefly before moving on to the next. That was the last thing she needed right now. John was a stalwart friend, someone she could count on through thick and thin. That was exactly what she did need, and her foolish, fluttering heart was just going to have to deal with it.

They went up the steps and paused in the double doorway. Like so many things here in Harland, the chapel looked pretty much the way it did in her memory. Something was different, though, and she couldn't quite put her finger on it.

"The roof was gone from here—" John pointed to the front corner "—most of the way back. Seth and the roofers decided to replace the whole thing. Then he and Lisa rebuilt the pews and the stage, refinishing them and the floor so everything matched up."

Impressive as all that was, Amanda's mind had hitched onto something else entirely. "You expanded it, too."

"Pastor Charles wanted to, but we couldn't afford that along with all the repairs. Maybe next year."

"That can't be right." Amanda studied the walls closely as she walked up the aisle. "It feels larger than I remember."

John chuckled. "That's funny. Usually when you go back somewhere you spent time in as a kid, the place feels smaller 'cause you're bigger."

He was right. It was a strange error to make, and she shook her head in confusion. Just then, a shaft of colored sunlight caught her eye, calling her attention to the beautiful stained-glass window just above the altar. During services, she'd often stared at the scene of Jesus surrounded by animals, admiring how the sun moved through the design to make gemlike prisms on the floorboards.

Unable to stop herself, she moved toward the window, drawn by something she couldn't begin to explain. Pausing in front of it, she examined it carefully, trying to figure out what had fascinated her all of a sudden. She'd seen that window a million times, and it hadn't affected her this way.

"You okay?" John asked from over her shoulder.

Still staring, she nodded. Apparently, that wasn't good enough, and he gently turned her to face him. "Are you sure? You look a little freaked out."

"I'm fine." Going up to the framed window, she said, "I just noticed something is all."

"Really?" he asked as he joined her. "What?"

"Look at this, back in the trees." She pointed to the shape she'd just discovered. "What does it look like to you?"

"I dunno. A shadow."

"A woman," she corrected him with certainty. "It's Mary."

Taking a step back, he tipped his head one way, then the other. "You think?"

"His mother was there, watching him with the animals. Isn't that sweet?"

"Sure."

His noncommittal response told her he still didn't see it, but she pressed. "Daniel Sawyer made this window, right?"

"They installed it in 1860, when they finished the church."

ou have any notes or anything?" she asked excitedly. "I mean, he must have had a plan for creating this. Have you ever seen it?"

"Far as I know, he just winged it."

"Nobody could possibly wing something this beautiful."

"He was a Sawyer," John reminded her proudly. "We leave the hard stuff up to God, then take what He gives us and make the most of it."

"You're saying God inspired Daniel to do this—" she waved at the window.

"That's what I'm saying."

"That's impossible."

"Oh, yeah?" Folding his arms, he tossed her a challenging grin. "Prove it."

Irritated by his smug expression, she shot back, "You prove yours."

Smiling, he looked at her as if she were a small child who needed short, uncomplicated words. "It's all about faith, Amanda. You either believe, or you don't."

"How can you be so sure about Him?"

"It's only fair," John replied quietly. "He's always been sure about me."

Leaving her no less bewildered than before, he turned and left her there in front of the window. When she checked again, the very feminine shadow was still there. If anything, she saw it more clearly than she had before. Was it a trick of the light, or did it mean something?

"Okay," she murmured. "I give up. What are you trying to tell me?"

She'd been away from religion for so long, she felt slightly ridiculous talking to a window. The crazy thing was, she felt a warm touch on her shoulder, as if someone had just put an arm around her. She got the strangest feeling that, despite her current predicament, everything would turn out fine.

Spooked by the odd encounter, she jerked herself back to her senses and hurried from the church.

Chapter Eight

It was finally the last day of school. Since she'd never been involved with children on a daily basis, Amanda had spent her first month in Harland struggling to keep up with the frantic end-of-school pace. Exams for Kyle, field trips for Emily, class parties and picnics, even a stint as Emily's show-and-tell project had left Amanda feeling more than a little wrung out.

The good news was that today marked the end of it all. In spite of everything she was going through with her pregnancy, Marianne had managed to plan a surprise celebration for the kids as a reward for doing so well in school. Of course, that meant Amanda was in on the whole thing, right down to picking up a special cake from Ruthy's Place.

When she pulled the van in alongside Harland's favorite diner, she smiled. Like all the other vintage buildings in town, this one had a quaint Southern charm. The cheerful blue-and-white-striped awning shaded several sets of wrought-iron bistro tables and chairs. The picturesque scene was made even more welcoming by the window boxes spilling over with ivy and flowers covering the spectrum from delicate baby's breath to bold-red geraniums.

As if that weren't enough, when she stepped onto the sidewalk, she was greeted by the unmistakable scent of fresh buttermilk biscuits and gravy. *If that didn't make your mouth water,* she mused as she opened the screen door, *you'd better check your pulse.*

The bells mounted over the door alerted everyone inside that she'd arrived, and most of the customers squinted at her with a total lack of recognition. Until the owner saw her, anyway.

"Amanda Gardner!" Wiping her hands on her no-nonsense bibbed apron, Ruth Benton hurried from the kitchen to wrap her in a hug. "I saw you at the Memorial Day gathering, and I've been wondering when you'd get around to coming in for a visit."

The petite woman held her away, assessing Amanda quickly. While the smile held, Amanda couldn't miss the disapproval in those cornflower-blue eyes. It reminded her of John's reaction to her when she first showed up at the farm, and she did her best to move past it.

"I've been so busy, I haven't had a chance." Settling on a stool, she propped her elbows on the old-fashioned lunch counter and rested her chin in her hands. "What's new?"

Ruthy laughed. "How long have you got?"

On her way into town, Amanda had prepared herself for a tongue lashing, which she probably deserved for staying away all these years and avoiding her hometown like the plague. It wasn't that she didn't want to visit, but after her parents moved away, she hadn't seen the point. It hadn't occurred to her that other folks in town would miss her, too.

Which made her think of John again. That had been happening more often than she was comfortable with, and she wished it would stop. Things were unsettling enough these days without constantly fending off thoughts of the devastatingly handsome farmer.

Ruthy poured two glasses of ice water and added a lemon wedge to each. "Since you're working out at the Sawyers', you must have met my nephew, Seth."

"I did. He and Lisa seem really happy."

Harland's number-one chef smiled fondly. "It's about time, I say. That boy has so much going for him, and he just needed the right woman to see it."

Ruthy added a nudging look, and Amanda frowned. "What?"

"There's more guys around here like my Seth." When Amanda didn't respond, she pressed. "On that farm, even."

Now she got it, and Amanda laughed. "Like John Sawyer, you mean."

"You said it, not me."

"We're friends, that's all."

"That's not what I saw on Memorial Day." Leaning in, Ruthy said quietly, "That man could snare any woman within twenty miles."

"And probably has," Amanda teased.

"He's the catch of the county, but none of his darlings stick around for long. Haven't you wondered why?"

"Because he's a hopeless slob and has relationship ADD?" When her smart-aleck comment got her nowhere, she shook her head. Ruthy was a notorious matchmaker, and while Amanda appreciated the attempt, it was doomed to failure. "John and I have always been good friends. You know that."

"Things change."

"Not this," Amanda insisted a little more forcefully. "John's a great guy, but he doesn't see me that way."

"I'll give you that one." Despite the concession, Ruthy's eyes crinkled with a knowing smile. "But how do *you* see *him,* peaches?"

"The same way." It was the honest truth, but Amanda felt her face getting warm. She knew that made her look like she was lying, but she couldn't help it. Her fair complexion had gotten her in trouble more than once.

Thankfully, Ruthy let it go and straightened up from her conspiring pose. "I'm guessing you're here for Marianne's cake."

Amanda blew out a quiet sigh of relief. "Yes, thanks."

When Ruthy brought it out of the cooler, Amanda *ooed.* "That looks amazing. I can't believe that pic of Kyle and Emily came out so well in frosting."

"Tell some people, would you?" Ruthy asked as she closed the lid of the box. "My daughter-in-law is home with their new baby, so she's trying to get this specialty baking business of hers going for some extra money. She thought with all the graduation parties and weddings coming up, it would be a good time to start, but it's not going well."

A struggling local business could be the answer to the question that had been plaguing Amanda for the last month: what would she do when the Collins family no longer needed a nanny?

"You know," she began, trying to keep her voice even, "while I was in California, I worked in marketing. I was pretty good at it."

Ruthy narrowed her eyes with interest. "I'm listening."

"What's your daughter-in-law's name?"

"Danielle."

"Does Danielle have a website?" Ruthy shook her head. "So people call her house phone when they want to order something?"

"Right."

"What exactly is specialty baking?"

"She makes custom cakes, pies, cookies, things like that," Ruthy explained. "Pictures, theme designs, whatever folks want. She was an art teacher, so she's very creative."

After a few more basic queries, Amanda decided that while Danielle Benton might be talented, she wasn't all that organized. That was common, especially among people whose businesses were based on something artistic like specialty baking. Whatever that was.

Which was the point, really. Danielle had to define what she did so she'd know who to market her products to. But she didn't know how, because nice, humble folks like her had no clue how to promote themselves.

"I've got an idea," Amanda suggested as casually as she could with her heart racing a mile a minute. "Why don't I sit down with her and see if there's something I could do to help her out? Maybe I can work with her to design a website that will spread the word about—what's the name of her company?"

Ruthy had caught on to where Amanda was coming from, and she chuckled. "She doesn't have one."

"Well, then, that's the first step." Taking a napkin out of the holder, she borrowed Ruthy's pen to scribble down Danielle's phone number. "I'll call her later and set up a meeting so we can talk about what she needs."

"She can't afford much," Ruthy cautioned.

"That's okay. I don't need much."

Just a chance, Amanda added silently as she picked up the cake and headed for the door. All she needed was one client, and then she'd be on her way.

"Did I miss supper?" John asked, knowing the answer before he finished the question.

Amanda was at the table, tapping away on a laptop, and she smiled. "Yes, but I saved you some ham. It's in the oven, on low."

"Man, you're the best. Is that Ridge's computer?"

"Yes. It was in Marianne's office, collecting dust. He traded it for a year's supply of snickerdoodles."

"Clever." On his way to the oven, he leaned in to kiss her cheek, but she shooed him off.

"Go away. I'm trying to set up my new PR company."

"Go away?" He gasped, staggering back melodramatically. "You're the first woman to ever say that to me."

"No doubt."

Chuckling, John let her be and poured a glass of sweet tea to go with the plate she'd left for him. Heaped with three thick slices of ham, mashed potatoes and buttermilk biscuits, all he had to do was pour some brown sugar glaze over the top and it was perfect.

"What's this about a new company?" he asked as he sat down across from her.

Folding her arms in front of the computer, she gave him a big, excited grin. "I'm going to start a promotions firm, focused on helping small businesses do websites and advertising to reach more customers. I've been cruising around the internet, trying to come up with a good name."

John swallowed a mouthful of potatoes. "You did all this since I saw you at breakfast?"

"Since I talked to Ruthy at the diner earlier." Amanda filled him in their conversation, obviously thrilled with the idea. "It's perfect for me. I'd be using everything I've learned about PR, but this time nobody can fire me because I'll be the boss."

The enthusiasm shining in her eyes was contagious, and John wanted to keep it going. "So, PR stands for what?"

"Public relations."

Sopping up melted butter with a biscuit, he suggested, "You could try using words that start with C-P-R. Y'know, like you're bringing them back to life or something."

"CPR," she repeated, circling her finger on the track pad with a pensive expression. After about ten seconds, she straightened up and started typing. When she was finished, she flashed him the biggest, brightest smile he'd seen since she'd come home. "Creative Promotional Resources. I just checked and I can get the domain *cpr4u.com*. It's jazzy, and folks will remember it."

Munching away, he nodded. "Cool. I like it."

"Really? Or are you just saying that because I'm pathetic and you feel sorry for me?"

"I don't feel sorry for you," John corrected her sternly. "Sure, you got shafted, but you're making the best of a bad hand. I don't pity folks like that. I admire them."

Eyes shining with joy, she looked at him as if he'd just told her she'd been crowned Miss America. "You admire me?"

"All the time."

Maybe a little more than he should, he had to admit as she got back to her computer and he finished his meal. Amanda might come across like a delicate rose, but beneath that classy, polished exterior of hers was a backbone of tempered steel. He hadn't recognized that when they were younger, but it was impossible to miss now.

It was one of the qualities forcing him to view his old friend in a new light. And it made him wonder if all these years he'd just been biding his time, waiting for her to grow up and come home.

Suddenly, the frantic tapping of keys stopped, and she sighed. "Rats."

"Don't tell me someone bought that name in the last two minutes."

"No, that's not it."

She didn't seem eager to share the problem, and John debated whether to push her. He'd been doing better letting her come to him, so he tamped down his natural impatience and focused on draining his glass and refilling it from the pitcher. Finally, he was rewarded.

"Bankruptcy is the worst," she confided with a heavy sigh.

"Is there some reason in particular you're saying that now?"

"I don't have a credit card, so I can't charge this purchase."

Her voice wavered, and he looked up to find

her fighting back tears. It felt like someone had driven an icicle into his heart, and John searched for a way to stem her emotions so he could keep a handle on his own.

Trying to look casual, he reached into the back pocket of his jeans and took out the worn-out wallet his father had given him for his high school graduation. John even had the original hundred-dollar bill, creased but safely tucked away in one of the pockets. In the slot beneath it was his one and only credit card. Without another thought, he removed the rarely used plastic and slid it across the table.

Amanda blinked at it a couple of times, as if she couldn't believe what she was seeing. When she lifted her gaze to his, she brought to mind a little girl who'd just gotten a pony for her birthday. "Seriously?"

"Sure." He shrugged. "Just don't go charging a Rolls or anything. My limit's not that high."

She looked down at the card, then at him again. "I don't know what to say."

Her gratitude warmed him right through, and he grinned. "You'd better get to it before some other smarty pants takes your idea."

Leaning over, she gave him a quick hug, then kissed his cheek. Now that it was her idea, she didn't seem to mind it so much. "Thank you, John. I'll pay you back, I promise."

"Don't worry about it."

"There's the setup fee and then monthly hosting," she informed him hesitantly. "I'll take it over as soon as I can, but it might be a while before I can get credit from anyone."

"No rush. I'm not going anywhere."

Rewarding him with another dazzling smile, she resumed her typing. In truth, he had no intention of letting her pay him back. She needed a hand, and he was glad to offer her one. But proud as she was, he knew she'd never accept charity, not even from him. He wanted to help, but he respected her independence even more.

Somehow, he'd figure out a way for them both to get what they wanted.

The Fourth of July was unusually quiet at the Sawyer farm. Because the health of Marianne and the twins was priority one, they voted to forgo their traditional picnic and keep things low-key.

They'd still taken the holiday off, so it had been a mellow day around the farm. Which meant Amanda had some rare time to herself. She was comfortably curled up on the front porch swing with a glass of lemonade and one of Marianne's homemaker magazines, trying to figure out where June had gone. Somehow, an entire month had whizzed by in a blur of housework, carpools and getting her fledgling company off the ground.

She'd spent her evenings designing a promotional plan and website for Danielle Benton, and profits for Dani's Delectables had been steadily picking up. There wasn't much money in it yet, but it was a start. Nowhere to go but up, Amanda told herself with a little grin.

The Collinses were all sprawled out with Marianne, enjoying a marathon of games from Chutes and Ladders to Monopoly. Frequent laughter filtered out from the living room, and Amanda smiled as she thumbed her way through the glossy pages. With her future slightly more in focus, it was easier for her to slow down and savor quiet moments like this.

Normally, she couldn't care less about the latest twenty-minute recipes or how to remove oil stains from denim. But now both were part of her job, and she was determined to master everything she needed to make her part of the Sawyer farm run smoothly. They'd gone out on a limb hiring her, she reasoned as she dog-eared a recipe for Jell-O cake. They deserved the best she could give them.

When Tucker plunked himself down at her feet, she looked up to find he wasn't alone.

"Hey there." Sitting at the other end of the

swing, John got it moving with a slight push of his feet. "Whatcha doin'?"

"Learning how to make Jell-O cake. How 'bout you?"

"Nothing." His eyes lit on her outfit, and he chuckled. "Going to yoga or something?"

Leave it to John to notice the oversize T-shirt and capris she was wearing. Rather than take offense, she decided to shrug it off. "I had half a day off, so I'm chilling."

She waited for him to bust her again, but he seemed to have lost interest in razzing her. Dropping his head back, he stared up at the roof beams and groaned. "I'm bored. Right about now, we're usually eating barbecue leftovers and cleaning up."

"Poor baby. There must be fireworks going on somewhere."

"Yeah." He sounded as enthusiastic as if she'd suggested he read *War and Peace* for amusement. "Up at the lake."

He punctuated the lackluster comment with the biggest sigh she'd ever heard, and she couldn't keep back a smile. He made her think of an antsy little boy hunting for something to do. "Why don't you call one of your girls and head out to watch the show?"

Since he didn't reject the notion immediately, she congratulated herself on coming up with a decent idea. When he turned to her, the mischief glinting in his eyes made her cautious. "What?"

"Wanna come out to the lake with me?"

"Me?" Bewildered, she shook her head. "Why me?"

"Why not you?" he countered, the glint broadening into that full-on country-boy grin. "Come on, Panda. It'll be fun."

"I don't know. Folks will talk."

"Who cares what they think?"

"I do."

"Since when?" he challenged. "You always did exactly what you wanted, no matter what anyone thought."

"That was a long time ago. Things have changed."

"Not in Harland," he reminded her. "Unlike the people you've been hanging out with in L.A., these folks actually like you."

John gave her one of those aggravating grins, and she felt herself wavering. Apparently, her foot-dragging was trying his patience, because he shrugged. "Okay. See ya later."

He stood and started toward the steps.

"You're still going?" She heard the whine in her voice, and it sickened her. She wasn't the kind of woman who connived to get a man's attention. What on earth was wrong with her?

Angling a glance back at her, he said, "Sure. It's a good idea."

"Yeah, it is." She couldn't remember the last time she'd done something spontaneous like that. Just went somewhere and enjoyed herself, for no reason other than it would be fun.

Pausing with one foot on the top step, the other on the next one down, he pinned her with the kind of look no mortal woman could resist.

"Knock it off, Sawyer. I'm immune, remember?"

In response, he cocked his head in a remarkable imitation of Tucker, and she couldn't help laughing. Marking her place in the magazine, she got to her feet. "All right, all right. I'm coming."

"Yeah." He gloated as he slung an arm over her shoulders. "I knew you would."

She elbowed him in the ribs, and he grunted but didn't move his arm.

"What was that for?" he asked, rubbing his side.

"For being you."

"But you love me," he argued as he slid open the end door of the barn.

"To a point. But I should warn you that I earned my black belt in jujitsu out in L.A. You'd do well to remember that tonight."

"Yes, ma'am."

Bowing, he motioned her to go ahead of him.

Once they were inside, he grinned in at her, eyes twinkling with a fondness she'd seen more frequently lately. She knew she was tempting fate by going out with him, but it had been so long since she'd had any fun, she decided she didn't care.

On the other side of the barn, a paint-spattered tarp covered her wreck of a car, and through the connecting door, she saw something that made her jaw drop. "Is that a plane?"

"That's Ridge's pride and joy, Ann Marie. He wanted to name her after Marianne, but she had a cow, so he switched it up. He and Kyle are restoring it."

A biplane, like the kind they used in old World War II movies, it was mostly in one piece, the exterior a patchwork of rust and body filler. Amanda wasn't mechanically inclined, but even she could see there was a gaping hole where the engine should be. "Where does he find time to work on it?"

"Here and there. He says it's almost done." John cast a dubious look at the plane. "I have to take his word on that."

Amanda laughed. "He seems like a good guy. Seth, too."

"They are, straight down to the ground. They fit right in around here."

She thought he was going to say something else, but apparently he changed his mind and headed for his beloved 1962 Triumph. She wasn't big on classic cars, so why she remembered the year escaped logic. Maybe because it had been important to him, that detail had stayed tucked in with the other cherished memories of her country boy.

"I can't believe you still have this thing." She ran a hand over the headrest on the passenger seat. The cracks in the leather were a little deeper, but she'd sat in that seat enough times to know it was the same one.

"I'm not done with it yet," he explained as he opened her door. "Matt and I just did a ton of frame-and bodywork, and the engine runs like clockwork. Now I'm working on the extras."

Glancing back, she noticed that the finish was mostly primer gray, with patches of several different kinds of red paint. She couldn't resist teasing him a little as he settled into the driver's seat. "I like the paint combo you've got going. Classy."

"Well, it's not a Mercedes or a Beemer, but I like it."

When he frowned, she realized she'd insulted him. Worse, she'd insulted his car, a major faux pas with any guy. Feeling bad, Amanda quickly said, "It's a fabulous car, John. I was only joking."

That seemed to soothe his wounded pride, and he started the engine. Easing the little convertible out of the barn, he headed up the driveway.

"I know it looks weird, but I can't pick a color from those little paint chips. I thought this would help me decide what works best."

"That makes sense."

In California, she'd driven nothing but convertibles, to take advantage of the nearly flawless weather. BMWs and Mercedes, as he'd mentioned, and her favorite—an almost intoxicating Porsche. She loved that car so much, she'd actually wept when it was repossessed and a flatbed came to take it away.

As the passenger, she felt obliged to make conversation. It was a good twenty minutes out to the lake, a long way to ride in silence. "Remind me where you got this again."

"Matt and I found it along the road when we were coming back from a Panthers game in Charlotte. The guy wanted a thousand, but I talked him into taking five hundred and an old dirt bike." Chuckling, he turned onto the highway. "I was only fifteen, and Dad was pretty steamed when we towed it home."

This was the first time he'd mentioned Ethan since that heart-wrenching night sitting under the tree with her. She had some idea how much he'd struggled to get to this point, and she was so proud, she could burst. If she called attention to it, she knew he'd shrug it off, so she stayed on the topic of his beloved little sports car.

"So you've been working on it all this time?" she asked.

"Yeah." Resting a hand on the cracked dashboard, he flashed Amanda his country-boy grin. "She's a lot of work, but she's worth it."

Amanda got the double meaning, and it settled nicely over her still-bruised heart. There was something about this guy, she thought, as she leaned back to admire the scenery flying by. No matter what happened, he somehow spun it to make it look manageable.

She wished she could do the same. With the turns her life had been taking, it would be a handy skill to have. "How's your soybean experiment going?"

"Pretty well. Everything's up, and the plants look healthy. I think," he added with a sheepish grin. "They're green, anyway."

Inspiration struck, and she almost heard a bell dinging in her mind. "Do you need some help promoting them?"

"Meaning would I hire CPR to do a website for the farm?"

"Meaning would you let CPR promote the farm for a year—no charge? It's the least I could do to pay you and your family back for all your help. I don't know what I would've done without it."

She heard the waver in her voice and swallowed hard to keep her composure. She'd gotten so accustomed to things going wrong, it was as if she couldn't handle it when they went her way for a change.

Apparently, John heard it, too, because he gave her that warm, you-can-count-on-me smile. "Sure. That'd be great."

Returning the smile, she rested her head back against the seat and closed her eyes. On a beautiful night like this, it was easy to envision the wind blowing her troubles away.

By the time they pulled into the lookout, Amanda was sound asleep. John had noticed her drifting the whole ride up here, and several times he'd considered heading back to the farm. It wasn't much past eight, but he figured the extra work for her new business must have worn her out. He didn't know how she did it, plucking ideas out of the air like that and making them real. It was amazing.

When the car stopped, she awakened with a start. Blinking a few times, she gave him a faint smile. "I guess I fell asleep."

"Yeah, you did." Something in her eyes made him wonder if there was another explanation. Yesterday, he'd have given anything to hear the whole story from her. Tonight she seemed so vulnerable, he hesitated to ask. "We can go home if you want. The lake'll be here all summer."

"No, that's fine." Raising her hands over her head, she stretched and looked around. "I'd forgotten how pretty this is."

John almost blurted out something remarkably similar about her, but he managed to stop himself. *Friends,* that annoying voice in his head reminded him. *Just friends.*

Because she liked country music, he tuned in a local station, and they stretched out on the hood of his car. With Amanda's head pillowed on his arm, the radio played softly behind them, blending with the scents of nearby cookouts and the warm night air. It was one of those simple things he loved, slowing down and staring at the sky. Of course, that he was here with Amanda tonight made it even better. While they chatted, the early stars began fading in like the opening scene of a movie.

"This is so cool," she breathed. "In L.A., there are so many lights we can't see the stars."

"What about Malibu?"

"Most nights, by the time I got home I was too exhausted to do anything but fall into bed."

John knew how that was, but he couldn't imagine going so long without getting a chance to do this. "So Ted wasn't into stargazing, then."

She let out a short, humorless laugh. "Hardly. The only stars he was interested in were on the red carpet."

"Too bad. Some folks just don't know how to enjoy themselves."

Stretching lazily, he caught the opening chords of an old song on the radio. Recognizing it instantly, he leaned over the windshield to turn up the volume.

"Wow," Amanda murmured with a nostalgic smile. "I haven't heard this in ages."

Sliding from the car, John reached back for her. When she took his hand, he reeled her into his arms to start a nice, slow dance.

Just the way she used to, she pillowed her cheek on his chest and sighed. "This is still my favorite song."

"Good to know."

Tilting her head to the side, she gazed up at him with sparkling eyes. "Whenever I hear it, I always think of you."

It had the same effect on him, but that wasn't the kind of thing he'd tell a woman he was dating. Treading too close to the romantic line would only get him in trouble later on.

Then again, this was Amanda. Judging by how he kept tripping over his heart, he was already in trouble with her. "Really? What goes through your head?"

"I wonder where you are, what you're doing. If you're happy," she added in a whisper laced with something he couldn't quite pinpoint. When her lips tipped up in an adoring smile, he completely lost his senses.

He leaned in and kissed her.

As soon as they connected, a baffling wave swept over him, nearly driving him to his knees. Because he'd acted on impulse, he didn't know what had possessed him to kiss her. But one thing he knew for certain.

He didn't want it to end.

Gathering her closer, he buried his face in the curve of her neck, drinking in the scent of coconuts that followed her everywhere. For a few incredible moments, they stood like that, not speaking, completely wrapped up in each other.

It was the single most perfect moment of his life.

When she burrowed into his chest, he knew she'd felt it, too. Reaching down, he tipped her chin up with the tip of his finger. The first shower of fireworks was reflected in her eyes, giving them more sparkle than ever. Brushing a stray curl from her cheek, he smiled. "This is way better than dancing under a disco ball."

That got him an adorable little pout. "You never kissed me back then."

"I know." Tracing the curve of her cheek with his finger, he finally voiced the feelings that had been plaguing him since the eventful day she unexpectedly dropped back into his life. "I always regretted that."

She laughed. "Really? Why?"

She thought he was joking, John realized. And why wouldn't she? He'd never given her a reason to take him seriously. "You were special."

"Right. Only one Panda." She mimicked him saying those same words, rolling her eyes with another laugh.

"That wasn't quite it." Wow, that was lame. From the very feminine smirk on her face, Amanda thought so, too.

"Then what was it?" Grabbing his hands, she playfully shook them. "Come on, Sawyer. We're all grown-up now, and I promise not to hold it against you."

Now was the time, his heart was screaming at him. If he didn't tell her the truth tonight, he never would. It was three words, he chided himself. The problem was he'd never said them to anyone, and he wasn't sure how she'd react. He didn't want to be the pathetic loser who floated them out there only to have them twisting in the air unreturned. Then again, someone had to be brave enough—or stupid enough—to say them first.

Framing her beautiful face in his hands, he watched as understanding dawned in her eyes. At that point, he suspected he didn't have to say anything. But he'd never done this before, and he wanted her to be the first woman to hear it from him.

"I love you, Amanda. I've always loved you."

As he ended his confession with a soft kiss, her lips trembled beneath his, and he felt her frowning under his thumbs. That wasn't the reaction he'd anticipated, and he wasn't sure what to think. When he broke their very intimate connection, she stiffened and pulled away, purposefully avoiding his eyes. He knew a defensive move when he saw one, and it took all his strength to draw his hands back and let her go. His feeling that something major was bothering her returned with a vengeance. This time, he didn't ignore it.

"Amanda."

At first, she refused to look at him. She wrapped her arms around herself and stared out at the lake. "Do you think they're going to put up any of those hissing white sparklers?"

When he quietly repeated her name, she squared her slender shoulders but still wouldn't face him. "What?"

"I know something's going on with you," he said gently. "I figured you'd tell me when you were ready, but you've been home more than a month now, and nothing. Maybe it's not as bad as you think."

"Oh, trust me," she retorted with a harsh laugh. "It is."

She wasn't crying, but her shaky voice told him she was on the verge of breaking down.

"Just tell me. We'll figure it out."

"No, we won't. There's no way to fix it."

She sounded so miserably certain, he was tempted to insist that she was dead wrong. Tell her that every problem had a solution, but he held back. What she needed was reassurance, not bullying, so he took a different tack. "You believed me when I said I love you, right?"

That got him a jerky nod, but nothing beyond that. It hadn't escaped him that she hadn't returned his sentiment, but he pushed aside his disappointment for now. "And if there's anything I can do to help you, I'll do it."

"You've already done so much." Finally turning, she gazed up at him with a watery smile. "I'm a grown-up now, John. I appreciate what you're saying, but there are some things I have to handle on my own."

The words were worrisome enough. The resigned tone of her voice put his protective instincts on full alert, and he gripped her shoulders gently. "That doesn't mean you have to carry the whole burden by yourself. I can take some of it, and then it'll be lighter for you. You just have to quit being so stubborn and let me do it."

Grimacing, Amanda folded her hands in front of her and stared down at them. "I'm pregnant."

Her revelation hit him like a sucker punch, and John absorbed it in shocked silence. Because he didn't want her to feel abandoned, he kept his hands lightly on her shoulders while he took in the full meaning of what she'd just told him.

This cleared up why she had a sudden aversion to coffee and a preference for bland oatmeal and plain toast. It explained why she wore a face mask when she was cleaning, and her strange reaction to Hailey. Amanda must not be sure how she felt about becoming a mother, and he couldn't blame her. He didn't want to say the wrong thing, so he held his tongue.

"I know it's awful," she said in a hushed, wavering tone. "That's why I couldn't go to my parents' place in Arizona. They're ashamed of me."

"Because you made a mistake?"

"Because I'm a—"

"Don't." He saw the word forming, and he stopped her with a finger over her lips. "Don't even think that. It's not true."

"I loved Ted," she confided, burying her face in John's chest with a sob. "I really, really did."

It was a good thing that two-timing snake was three thousand miles away. If John ever ran across him, he'd be sorely tempted to strangle the coward with his bare hands. While he wasn't crazy about her being in love with someone that slimy, John decided that was why she hadn't said she loved him, too.

At least not yet, a hopeful voice whispered in the back of his mind.

Once Amanda settled a little, she lifted her head and met his gaze. Her eyes were a flat, miserable blue, and he searched for a way to bring the light back into them.

"This baby is Ted's responsibility, too," he said angrily. "He wouldn't help you?"

The tactic worked like a charm, and she snorted in disgust. "He offered to pay to 'take care of it.'" Temporarily back to her spunky self, she air-quoted the last few words with disdain. "If I went along, he promised I'd never want for anything ever again."

"To make sure you kept your mouth shut about the affair."

"That was his style."

"I'm no lawyer, but I think they call that blackmail." Several insults came to mind, but John decided they were better left unsaid. "You're better off without him."

"I know." Despite her flash of bravado, Amanda focused on him with a desperate expression. "Please don't tell anyone."

John understood her request, but it wasn't in

his nature to be anything but honest, especially with his family. "How far along are you?"

"My doctor in California said the baby's due around Thanksgiving. On Saturday, I have an appointment to meet my new doctor. I talked to her on the phone, and she sounds really nice. Understanding."

"Meaning you want me to be understanding, too?"

"Please, John. You're the only one who knows, and I want to keep it that way."

Giving him an expectant look, she cranked the wattage on those irresistible baby blues. Even though he questioned the wisdom of agreeing, he didn't know what she'd do if he insisted she come clean with his family. Jittery as she seemed right now, he wouldn't be surprised if she quit her job and left the farm rather than confide what she obviously felt was an unforgivable mistake.

That would leave the Sawyers without a housekeeper, and Amanda on her own with no money, no job and no car. In his mind, all those options were worse than keeping his mouth shut a little longer. Beyond that, he'd never had much success refusing her anything. He really shouldn't continue letting her run roughshod over him this way, but old habits die hard. At least, that was the excuse he gave himself as he reluctantly nodded.

"Okay. For *now,*" he clarified sternly.

"Thank you." Gratitude flooded her eyes, and she rewarded him with an exuberant hug.

Returning that warm gesture felt so natural, he did it without thinking. He came dangerously close to kissing her again, then thought better of it. She was still in trouble, and while he could be supportive, it would be best for both of them if he kept his distance.

He couldn't care less what other folks might think, but she had enough going on in her life right now without adding him to the mix. She knew he loved her, but he wouldn't be surprised to find she wasn't ready to even think about getting involved with someone while carting around such life-altering baggage.

It made every kind of sense, John reasoned. He'd just have to be patient while she sorted things out. And he'd try not to think about what he'd do if she never said those precious words back to him.

Pushing the unfamiliar emotions aside, he got practical. "You know you can't keep a secret like this forever, right?"

"I'll deal with that later." With a determined look, she added, "Marianne's twins are due in a few weeks, and I figure she'll be back on her feet by early September. By then I'll have some money to tide me over until CPR starts turning a profit, and I can get my own place."

"Where?"

"I was thinking Kenwood. It's bigger than Harland, and people there don't know me."

"That's the problem," he pressed. "You'll be even more pregnant then, and things will only get harder. Do you really want to be on your own like that?"

"I'm tougher than I look," she assured him airily. "I'll be fine."

"How 'bout after the baby's born? It takes both Matt and Caty to take care of Hailey when she's healthy, never mind when she's sick. How are you gonna manage that and work full-time?"

He managed to stop short of begging her to stay at the farm, but just barely. Judging by her sudden dive in attitude, she hadn't planned that far ahead. Even when they were kids Amanda had always been a dreamer, jumping from one adventure to another without looking. In truth, her bold, spontaneous nature was one of the things he'd admired most about her. That is, until she left her easygoing buddy behind and flew off to find her rainbow. He hadn't liked that much. And now that she had a child to consider, that kind of impulsiveness could lead them both straight into disaster.

For a few moments, she looked even less confident than she had earlier, and John regretted voicing his concerns so bluntly. Judging by her reaction, he suspected that she'd had the same thoughts but for some crazy reason had tucked them away to examine later. The problem was, Thanksgiving wasn't as far away as she seemed to think. She had a lot to figure out between now and then.

John Sawyer was in love with her.

Hugging her pillow, Amanda allowed herself to savor the memory of their first kiss for a few blissful moments. Dancing to that song, with the fireworks going off over the lake, had been like a scene from a romantic movie. The kind where the guy tells the girl he's been in love with her forever, and she gasps in surprise and tells him she's always loved him, too.

Only that's not how it went for her, Amanda recalled with a sigh. Because she was too scared to bring John that close, only to have him decide that she *and* a baby were more than he'd bargained for. Men liked to make their own children, she mused sadly, not inherit someone else's.

Still, she couldn't believe it had never occurred to her that John had such strong feelings for her. It explained why he'd always been her champion, defending her from boys who got out of line. From high school to the present, he'd come to her rescue time after time, never too busy— or too angry—to make sure she was okay. It also cleared up that pesky question Ruthy had asked her at the diner.

He's the catch of the county, but none of his darlings stick around for long. Haven't you wondered why?

Now Amanda understood it was because John loved her. Not Ginger, or one of the countless cheerleaders he'd dated in high school who still probably lived around here. Her. Driven, high-maintenance, demanding her.

Just thinking about it made her giddy, as if she'd won first prize in a contest she hadn't even entered. As she snuggled into that feeling, she realized that she felt the same way about him. It was why he'd kept crossing her mind every so often, even though he was thousands of miles away. She'd always assumed it was a simple case of nostalgia, revisiting her country boy when life in the fast lane got to be too much to handle.

Now she recognized that John had represented much more than a safe haven from adult responsibilities. Somehow, her heart had known that he was the one man she could trust never to hurt her. The one who would always step between her and the world, no matter what nasty turns her life might take. She hadn't come back to Harland for a fresh start in friendly territory.

She'd come back to John.

And, as always, he hadn't let her down. Despite his resentment over her neglecting him, he'd come around and done more to help her than she ever could have expected. Because he loved her.

But how did he feel now? she wondered, resting her hand over the noticeable bulge under her oversize T-shirt. Was his immense heart generous enough to love her in spite of the fact that she was carrying another man's child?

Or had she finally done something so horrible that even John couldn't forgive her?

Lying there in the dark, she did something she hadn't done in a very long time.

"Please, God," she whispered as tears started down her cheeks. "I know I don't deserve it, but if you're still listening to me, I could really use your help."

In the early morning hours, John lay awake, staring up at the ceiling. He'd been doing a lot of that lately, and it didn't take a brain surgeon to diagnose the reason.

Amanda.

Now that he knew what she'd been keeping from him, part of him wished he hadn't pushed to know the truth. Then again, it wouldn't be much longer before everyone in town figured it out, and then he'd be mad that she hadn't trusted him enough to confide in him herself. Right?

He didn't even want to think about the tangled

feelings that had wrapped around him, refusing to let go. One thing he couldn't deny: Amanda hadn't suddenly gotten under his skin tonight at the lake. She'd stolen his heart in high school, but he'd been too dense to realize it. Now, when there might actually be something between them, the timing couldn't possibly be worse.

Rubbing his hands over his face, he groaned at the knotted thoughts clogging his mind. From Ted's callous attitude toward an innocent unborn child, to the Gardners' cold rejection of their own daughter, John found himself swirling in a sea of rage totally foreign to him. Having lost his mother when he was only five, he accepted that life wasn't fair, that things didn't always work out the way he wanted them to.

God had reasons for doing what He did, and John had always trusted in that wisdom without question. But this time, Amanda was caught up in the mess, and he wasn't taking it well.

"Why?" he said out loud. "I know she's not close to You right now, but she's a good person, and she doesn't deserve to have all this bad stuff happening. Why would You let her get hurt over and over like this?"

While he mulled it over some more, it dawned on John that he'd answered his own question. In truth, God hadn't let Amanda drift away from Him unnoticed. When her life spiraled out of control, He took the opportunity to send her back to Harland where she belonged.

And to him, John realized with sudden clarity. Because, difficult as it would be, he wouldn't abandon her now. Amanda might claim all kinds of toughness, but he suspected that she and her baby were going to need all the love and understanding he could give them.

Just before he fell asleep, he closed his eyes and prayed for strength. For all of them.

Chapter Nine

Was the Sawyer kitchen *ever* completely empty? Amanda wondered while she cracked eggs for omelets Saturday morning. John and Matt were there, breaking up a day that had started before dawn with a farmer's breakfast. Caty was filling a bottle for Hailey while the little cherub blew raspberries at her daddy. Ridge, Kyle and Emily stopped just long enough for some cereal and orange juice before heading out to Kyle's baseball game.

As the van went up the driveway, Amanda realized she had no way to get into town until they came back. Glancing at the clock, she saw that it was nine. "When is baseball over?"

"Two, maybe three," John mumbled around a mouthful of eggs. "Doubleheader today."

Caty was the first one to figure out what she really meant. "Do you need the van?"

Much as Amanda hated to cancel her appointment, she saw no way around it. "It can wait, I guess. Matt, did you have a chance to look at my car?"

Since he was chewing, he nodded. After a sip of coffee, he replied, "My advice? Call a wrecker."

More bad news, Amanda thought as she bit her lip. "It's as bad as all that?"

"If it was ten years newer, I'd take a shot at it just for fun. Main problem is, all those fried parts are gonna be tough to find."

"Which makes them expensive," she guessed.

"Yup. Junkyard's the best place for that stuff, but it takes a long time to find something in good enough shape to use. The scrapyard will come and get the car, give you seventy-five bucks or so and get it out of here."

Nice as he was being about the whole thing, it didn't take a genius to read between the lines: please get your wreck of a car out of my barn. "Okay, I'll call them Monday."

"That doesn't solve your problem today," Caty pointed out. "You can use Matt's truck if you want."

"Sorry, I have to get more seed this morning," Matt corrected his wife. "What about John's car?"

John broke up laughing, making Amanda smile. "I don't know how to drive a standard."

"You're kidding." She shook her head, and

Matt said, "Well, I can go later. Go ahead and take my truck."

"That'll set us behind another half day, and we're already a week behind," John reminded him. "I'll take her and then come back."

He'd obviously decided he was accompanying her to the doctor, and Amanda's pulse spiked with dread. She was nervous enough without bringing along a spectator. Especially not one who'd bared his soul to her one night and gave no sign of it the following morning. His bizarre attitude was making her edgier than she'd have imagined was humanly possible. "You don't have to—"

"No problem. Really." Punctuating the final word with a "don't argue with me" look, he shoved his chair back and stood. "I've got some things to do on the way. Let's go."

"I'm not ready." Appalled by the shake in her voice, Amanda wanted nothing more than to crawl back under the covers and go back to sleep.

"Yeah, you are." Opening the door, he repeated, "Let's go."

Her feet felt like they were cemented to the floor. Caty's puzzled expression got her in gear, and Amanda gave herself an internal shake. Forcing herself to move, she got her purse from a hook in the pantry and managed a reasonably calm goodbye.

"Thanks for nothing," she muttered to John as

they strolled toward his car parked in the turn-around. "This is really hard, you know."

"Putting it off won't make it any better."

"Easy for you to say."

"The Kenwood Clinic, right?" he asked as he opened the passenger door for her. "So nobody in town will see you going."

"Am I really that predictable?"

"You're very unpredictable. I just know how your mind works."

They stood there, at arm's length, staring at each other. For the first time she could recall, she couldn't read John's feelings in his eyes. They were guarded, studying her the way they had the day she showed up at the farm. Hesitant, mistrustful.

"John, about last night—"

He waved her off before she could finish. "Don't worry about it. Lost my head is all."

She'd lost hers right along with him, forgetting about everything but how it felt to be wrapped in his arms, bathed in starlight and fireworks, drinking in the moment. Wishing it would go on forever.

Tell him, her heart whispered. *Tell him you love him.*

Torn between sentiment and practicality, she gazed up at him, hoping he might somehow understand. Slowly, the ice in his eyes warmed to the color of a clear summer sky, and he gave her a tender smile. "I'm not Ted, y'know. When I say 'I love you,' I mean it."

"How did you know that's what was bothering me?" she asked with a shaky laugh. "Even I didn't know until just now."

"I told you." Reeling her into his arms, he dropped in for a quick kiss that was half smirk. "I know how your mind works. What I'm interested in now is what you're feeling."

As the last of her misgivings fell away, her answer came easily. "I love you, too."

During her long, sleepless night, she'd realized it was true. She'd loved the boy, and now the man he'd become. It had happened so gradually, she hadn't recognized her enduring fondness for what it really was: a deep, unshakable love that had already lasted for years. Impossible as that seemed to her, when it came to John, she just couldn't help herself.

Hooking her thumbs onto his thick leather belt, she smiled up at him. "You know that."

"I still like hearing it."

"Things are bound to get really tough. With everything else you've got, why would you want to take on a pregnant woman?"

"Because I love this pregnant woman." Smiling reassurance, he rested his strong hand on her waist. "And I love kids in general, so this is no big deal. I'm your guy, Amanda. I won't let you down."

In the middle of a long, lazy kiss, it occurred to her that anyone could see into the barn, and she pulled away. "This is a really bad idea."

"Why?"

"Anyone can see us in here."

Laughing, he tickled her nose with his finger. "You really have to quit fretting over what people think."

His condescending tone irked her, and she narrowed her eyes in irritation. "Care to guess what I'm thinking right now?"

Stepping back, he motioned her into the car. "I'd rather not put it into words. It's rude."

He was completely right, and despite her annoyance she had to laugh. "I'm not sure how I feel about that. I never know what you're thinking."

"Don't worry, Panda," he assured her as he started the engine. "When you need to know, I'll tell you."

John sat in the obstetrics waiting room, the only guy among a dozen or so women. And girls, he noticed with a frown. Some of them didn't look old enough to drive on their own at night. Where were the boys who got them this way? he wondered angrily. If you were old enough to create a life, you were old enough to take responsibility for your child.

That led him straight back to thinking about the selfish Ted. He not only cheated on his wife and lied to Amanda, but he wanted to pay her to end a life that had every right to continue. Forgiving by nature, John was human enough to believe that Ted deserved whatever disasters fell on him.

This was the last time he'd think about it, John promised himself as he stood to give his seat to a very pregnant woman with a toddler in tow.

"Oh, bless you." As she and her little boy sat down, she gave John a faint smile. "I'm just about ready to drop."

She looked it, but John kept his opinion to himself and grinned back. "No problem. I could use a stretch, anyway."

"My husband usually comes with us." Reaching into a bag for a coloring book and crayons, she handed them to her son. "But he had to work."

Noting that she wore a gold band on the chain around her neck, John assumed her comment about having a husband was for the benefit of anyone listening. He couldn't help wondering how Amanda would handle that kind of thing. Some Harland folks were open-minded about single moms, some not so much. Considering her proud nature and breakneck personality, she'd need every ounce of courage she had just to walk down the street.

Amanda's situation made him view this stranger with more sympathy than usual. When she placed a hand on her stomach and winced, he hunkered down beside her. "Can I get you anything?"

A doctor, maybe?

Obviously in pain, she gritted her teeth and shook her head. When the spasm passed, she sighed. "Just some Braxton-Hicks contractions—nothing to worry about."

"O-kay." She sounded like she knew what she was talking about, but he didn't feel right leaving her alone. "I'm John Sawyer, by the way."

"Melinda Reed," she breathed. "Nice to meet you."

"Can I get you some water or something?"

"That would be great. Thank you."

He filled two cups from the watercooler, handing one to her and the other to her son. She thanked him again just as a nurse appeared in the open doorway.

"John Sawyer?"

Jumping to his feet, he almost knocked over three plastic kids' chairs. "Yes, ma'am."

"Calm down." She added an understanding smile. "And follow me."

"Is everything okay?" he asked as they walked down a hallway between a dozen closed doors.

"Just fine. Amanda wanted you to see something."

Being more or less clueless about pregnancy, he wasn't sure he was ready for any of this. *Man up,* he chided himself. It's not like he was the one having the baby. How bad could it be?

The nurse opened one door that looked like all the others, except Amanda was on the other side. Lying on a table in front of a computer screen, she smiled and held her hand out to him. "Come and meet my daughter."

Stunned beyond belief, for a second he couldn't move. When her joyful smile began to droop, John forced himself to go in and take her hand. With the other she pointed at the screen, where he saw a blob he couldn't have identified as human if he tried. As he watched, it actually moved a little, and he registered a low drumming sound.

"Is that your heartbeat?" he asked Amanda.

"No." Eyes shining with excitement, she squeezed his hand tighter. "It's hers. My daughter's."

He felt the kick in her pulse as she said those words, and he had no idea what to make of it. Her reaction was a complete turnaround from the very pragmatic view she'd had of her situation until this moment. The change in her attitude was bewildering, and he covered his uneasiness by studying the wavering image on the screen.

A baby, his brain insisted, although it was kind of hard to tell. Amanda's baby. This child wasn't his, wasn't even remotely his responsibility. But John knew himself pretty well, and he suspected that if this little girl ever asked him for anything, he'd lay himself out flat to give it to her.

Just as he'd always done with her mother, he realized with an inward groan. While he hated to even think about it, his instincts told him his carefree days were over.

When Amanda entered the waiting room, she found John surrounded by women. As usual, she thought with a mental eye roll. He was a Sawyer boy, after all. Impossible as it seemed, he couldn't help being irresistible.

"John, are you flirting with the patients?"

As Amanda joined them, one of the moms-to-be smiled up at her. "He was helping, not flirting. Your husband is very sweet."

Amanda almost corrected her, then decided it might be smarter to let the misunderstanding go. This pregnancy would be trying enough without her blurting out to every stranger she met that she wasn't married.

Apparently reading her mood, John stood to his full, very solid height. "Ready to go?"

"Very."

The lengthy exam and endless questions had been aggravating, and she was worn out. Listing the details of her family's medical history—high blood pressure, heart attacks, strokes—had been more than a little depressing. When it came to her mother's pregnancies, she had no clue because they didn't talk about things like that. Considering that their last conversation had ended with some very personal insults and an abrupt click, Amanda wasn't keen on calling to ask Mom to fill in the blanks. So she was on her own.

The morning's only saving grace was the sonogram picture she had tucked in her purse. *Her daughter,* she thought mistily while John started the car. It was almost too much for her to process.

Closing her eyes, she rested her head back against the seat and focused on the wind rustling through her hair, the warmth of the sun on her face. When she felt the car slow and stop, she rolled her head to look over at John.

Shutting off the engine, he swiveled and put a hand on the back of her seat, the way he used to. The sweet memory popped up all on its own, making her current predicament seem even worse by comparison. Tears welled in her eyes, and she blinked to keep them contained. Hormones, the doctor had explained. What a pain.

John responded by brushing a thumb across

her cheek. "Talk to me, Amanda. Tell me what's going on in that pretty head of yours."

It had been forever since someone had spoken to her so tenderly, and it made her smile. "How much time have you got?"

"How much do you need?"

The question struck her as a reflex, proving just how different John was from Ted. Generous and caring, ignoring the pile of work waiting for him back at the farm because she needed him. This wonderful man cared about other people, and would go out of his way to help them if he could.

And he loved her. He'd not only said it, he'd shown her, over and over. If she could trust anyone to understand, it would be him.

"I'm scared, John," she confided in a whisper.

He scowled at that. "What did the doctor say?"

"Oh, the baby and I are fine." She waved away his concern. "I just don't know what to expect. I got a book about pregnancy, so I'm okay on most of that. But none of my friends had children, so when it comes to babies, I'm a little lost."

"You could talk to Caty and Marianne."

Disgusted by her utter lack of knowledge, she groaned. "I'm so clueless, I wouldn't know what to ask."

"Then it's a good thing I got this."

To her surprise, he reached behind the seat and

handed her a plain white plastic bag. Opening it, she pulled out a copy of a book with a woman holding a baby on the cover. She looked so happy, smiling out at the reader, projecting the idea that impending motherhood was a good thing. Checking the bag again, Amanda noticed there was another copy.

"They had 'em in the shop at the clinic," he explained. "I got one for you and one for me. Y'know, so we can be ready for what's coming."

His thoughtful gesture played on her unpredictable emotions, and she swallowed hard to keep back a rush of tears. "That was really sweet. Thank you."

"I read some while I was waiting." He started the engine and pulled back onto the road. "It says being extra emotional is normal." Glancing over, he grinned. "Just don't push it."

Laughing, she shook her head. "How is it you always know how to make me laugh?"

"It's a gift," he said, echoing the comment she'd made to him on her first day back.

So she repeated his snotty comeback. "If you say so."

They both laughed at that one, and John asked, "Have you thought of any names yet?"

"I think I'll wait until she's born. Then I'll know if she looks more like a Sophia or a Karen."

"Makes sense, I guess. Are you hungry?"

"Starving," she replied immediately. "I was so nervous about my appointment, I couldn't eat a thing at breakfast."

"Ruthy's?"

Just hearing the name of Harland's blue-ribbon chef made her mouth water. "That sounds fabulous."

"We can get caught up on all the gossip while we're there. I'm pretty much stuck on the farm this time of year, so I miss a lot."

"Even if you weren't, you wouldn't know anything. You're too busy chasing women to hear much."

"For the record, Sawyer boys don't chase women." Glancing over, he gave her a shameless grin. "They chase us."

Amanda hooted at that. "I can't imagine Caty Lee McKenzie chasing after Matt for one second. She's way too smart for that."

"Yeah, well, she's an exception. So are you."

The warmth in his voice soothed her frayed nerves, and she sat back to enjoy the ride.

When John pulled onto Main Street in Harland, Ruthy's Place pulled him in like a beacon in the middle of the town's small business district. He adored the owner, but if he was honest, the fact that she made the best pies in three counties probably had something to do with that.

"You'd best watch yourself with Ruthy," he warned Amanda as he opened the passenger door. "It's hard to keep secrets from her."

"Whatever. Right now I'm too hungry to care."

Shrugging, he pulled open the antique glass door to let her go through. There were a few people in line ahead of them, and Amanda scoped out the dining room with a nostalgic smile. Glancing up, she said, "That wall didn't have any knick-knacks when I was here in June. Who put that shelf up?"

"Seth built it for her. Said next time they'll have to add a new row under the old one."

"It must take her hours to dust all that stuff."

John chuckled. "Listen to you, sounding all domestic."

"Impressed?" she asked with a cute smirk.

The lighter mood was a huge improvement over her earlier frame of mind, and he wanted to keep it going. "Definitely. I didn't know you had it in you."

A mischievous gleam lit her eyes. "I'm just full of surprises."

"Good to know."

"Amanda!" Ruthy called out, hurrying from behind the counter to fold her into a warm embrace. Holding Amanda at arm's length, she asked, "How's the PR business?"

"So far, Danielle's my only client. She said her orders have picked up, though."

"Her phone's been ringing off the hook since you did that emailing. I've had my hands full helping her keep up."

"That's great news. The website revisions are almost ready. If she likes what I've done, it'll go live on Monday."

"It sounds like things are rolling right along," Ruthy continued, handing them each a menu.

They chatted back and forth for a few minutes, and John marveled at her ability to talk with Ruthy without revealing a single detail about anything. Caty and his sisters were adept at that, too. It must be a woman thing, he decided while he checked out the specials board.

His reprieve didn't last, though. Before long, Ruthy's sharp eyes landed on him. "And what about you? Last I heard, you were dating the new gym teacher."

"Over the winter, I was. Now it's summer."

"Oh, you're terrible," she scolded, smacking his shoulder. "I thought with Matt settled down, you might decide it looked good to you, too."

"I might." Grinning, John winked at her. "You never know."

"Don't you try that on me. Gus would have your head."

"Gus?" Amanda repeated. "Gus Williams, the owner of Harland Hardware?"

"The same." Ruthy's eyes sparkled, and she proudly displayed her left hand. Dusted with flour, it sported an impressive circle of emeralds. "He flew all the way to Dublin to get this from an antiques dealer he knows. We got married on St. Patrick's Day."

"That's wonderful! Congratulations."

"John didn't tell you?"

"I wanted to let you tell her," he explained. "You enjoy doing it so much."

"That's true enough. I've got a fresh batch of sweet tea. Would you like some while you look at your menus?"

John agreed, but Amanda shook her head. "Water for me, thanks."

Ruthy's puzzled look lasted less than a second, telling John her instincts were as bang-on as ever. After she'd left them alone, he leaned in to avoid anyone overhearing. "She knows, Panda."

"I doubt that," Amanda scoffed as she opened her menu. "I know everyone around here thinks she's psychic or something, but she's not."

But when Ruthy brought her a little plate of soup crackers to go with her water, Amanda gave John a long, wry look. Once they'd placed their orders, she laughed. "Sorry. I guess you were right."

"After Mom died when we were kids, Ruthy sort of became our fairy godmother. Y'know, looking after us and Dad, making sure things got done around the house." He pointed at the ceiling. "Those apartments she keeps upstairs, she lets folks use 'em for free until they're back on their feet. She's got a knack for reading people, and knowing what they need. Sometimes before they know it themselves."

Amanda's gaze drifted upward, and it didn't take a genius to figure out what was going on in that quick mind of hers. John wasn't keen on her leaving the farm to fend for herself, but in the end it was her decision. At least here Ruthy would watch out for her.

Popping a couple of the small crackers into her mouth, Amanda chased them with water. "I guess I was too young to appreciate all that before."

"Nothing had gone wrong for you yet. You don't pick up on that stuff until things go haywire."

"You're right." She made a sour face. "I guess I'm making up for it now."

John wasn't big on lectures, whether he was on the giving or receiving end. Feeling dangerously close to sounding preachy, he decided to switch tracks and lighten things up at little. "Would you like to do something tonight?"

"Like what?"

He shrugged. "I've gotta help Matt bale hay this afternoon, but maybe you and I could catch a movie."

She flashed him the megawatt smile he remembered from high school. "That sounds like fun. Thanks for asking."

Chapter Ten

Amanda fell asleep halfway through the movie, and John razzed her about it until she had to smack him. Sunday morning, their eventful day was still fresh in her mind, and she'd come to terms with something that hadn't been in her plans when she decided to return to Harland.

John was standing by her. Even though she was carrying another man's baby, and he clearly didn't approve of what she'd done. Despite his personal feelings, John wouldn't let her flounder through this pregnancy on her own. While he acknowledged her mistake, he hadn't judged her for it, hadn't turned his back on her when she'd finally dredged up the courage to tell him the truth.

Finding out that he'd loved her all these years was a wonderful bonus.

Was it Harland, with its small-town values, that had made him that way? Or was it his family, who had always supported each other through thick and thin? Or was it simply that John was born to be a solid, stand-up kind of guy a girl could depend on when she needed him?

Whatever the reason, Amanda mused as she took her egg-and-sausage casserole from the fridge, she was grateful that he'd finally agreed to keep her secret as long as possible. The next few months would be difficult, at best, and she'd need all the help she could get. When she reached into the cupboard over the stove for the frame that went with the casserole dish, a hand appeared from behind her and plucked it free.

"Got it," John said, handing it to her.

"I can reach."

"I can reach easier." Grinning, he tickled her nose with his finger, probably because he knew it drove her crazy.

"You need to stop. If you keep babying me, your family's going to figure things out."

"Not likely." Leaning in, he murmured, "But maybe you should be up front with people instead of letting them figure it out on their own. They might surprise you," he added with a meaningful look at the happy group gathered around the table.

"I'll take my chances."

He frowned, and she braced herself for an argument. She hated being at odds with him over this, but she firmly stood her ground.

"They're my family." He deftly played the emotion card. "I'm not in the habit of keeping stuff from them."

"Fine. Tell them. I don't care."

Cocking his head, he gave her a suspicious look. "But you'll never make me pancakes again."

"Trust me." She elbowed past him to the oven. "That will be the least of your problems."

He didn't say another word, but he straightened to his full, very intimidating height and glowered down at her. Knowing how much he loved her, Amanda felt awful for putting him in the position of basically choosing between her and his family.

John didn't respond, brushing past her on his way to the table. Disgusted with herself for being a coward, she slid the casserole into the oven and set the timer.

When he called her name, she scowled at him. "What?"

"I hate to criticize, seeing as I'm no expert in the kitchen like you."

"Spit it out, Sawyer."

Cocking one amused eyebrow, he nodded toward the stove. "You might want to turn it on."

Sure enough, the oven dial was still at Off. She spun it to the right temperature and stubbornly avoided looking at John. Which was difficult, because he was doing everything in his power to annoy her. Spreading the paper all over the table, feeding Tucker bacon from his own plate. The kicker was when he pointed his fork at Ridge and said, "I can out arm wrestle you, flyboy."

"In your dreams, son." At a warning look from his wife, the pilot-turned-farmer backtracked. "Later."

John shrugged, then winked over at Amanda. She wouldn't have noticed if she hadn't been watching him, she reminded herself in frustration. It wasn't bad enough that he looked better than usual, dressed in nice chinos and a button-down for church. Did he have to push every button she had?

The doctor had advised her that she'd be more edgy than normal. But Amanda had to acknowledge there was no reason to make things any worse for herself—and for John—than they had to be.

She took a deep breath, thought once more, and said, "There's something I need to tell all of you."

Everyone looked up expectantly, and she felt the impact of ten sets of eyes. Eleven if you counted Tucker, who sat and wagged his tail, hoping she had a treat for him. She'd expected to do this alone, spotlighted and terrified in front of a family that had all but adopted her not once, but twice.

To her surprise, John stood and pulled out a chair for her at the table. Then he sat down and backed away so they could see her but he was still close enough to offer moral support. That wordless, protective gesture almost did her in, and she swallowed hard so her voice would hold steady while she told her tragic tale. Out of respect for the kids, she left out the most unsavory details, presuming the adults were perfectly capable of filling in the blanks.

Emily, of all people, summed it up best. Turning to Marianne, she said, "Mommy, Amanda's having a baby, too. Isn't that great?"

"Babies are gifts straight from Heaven," Marianne agreed, smiling as she reached over to give Amanda's hand a warm squeeze. "Every one of them is special."

"I'm confused." Kyle frowned. "Will Amanda's baby be our cousin like Hailey is?"

"No," Amanda answered quickly, "but you can all be really good friends."

She chanced a look over at John, whose proud smile was all the approval she needed. Finally, after struggling for so long, things were looking up for her. It wasn't an accident, she understood with sudden clarity. She'd turned her back on God, but He hadn't forgotten about her. The ghostly image in the church window wasn't her imagination. In her heart, she knew God had seen her standing there and sent her a real, honest-to-goodness sign, welcoming her into His house if she wanted to return. Even before her desperate plea for help, He'd been watching her, waiting for her to come around.

Belated gratitude flooded through her, and she heard herself say, "I think I'll go to church with all of you today."

Silence. The adults looked at each other, then over at her as if they couldn't believe they'd heard right. The delighted expression on John's face made it all worthwhile.

"That's awesome, Panda. Folks'll be real glad to have you there."

"I hope so."

Taking her hand, he closed it inside his in a reassuring gesture. "Even if they're not, we will be."

While his family echoed the sentiment, John's eyes glowed with admiration. Amanda felt as if an elephant had been lifted off her shoulders, and she found herself looking forward to Pastor Charles's Sunday service.

Waiting for everyone to get ready to leave, John debated whether to ask the question that had been bugging him since Amanda dropped her baby bombshell. Finally, when the two of them were pulling in at the church, he decided to go for it. "What changed your mind?"

"About coming clean with your family or going to church?" she parried with a smile.

"Both."

"Actually, it was the sonogram yesterday. Up until that point, being pregnant was a problem I had to deal with." A soft smile played over her features as she rested a hand on her stomach. "Now she's real, and people should know about her."

"And the church thing?"

"The same reason, I guess." She gazed out at the people filing in for Sunday service, then over at him. "I never really believed in miracles until yesterday."

"Yeah, it's pretty amazing. I remember seeing Caty and Marianne's pictures—how proud Matt and Ridge were." Reaching over, he took Amanda's hand loosely in his. "I'll help however I can. We all will."

Lacing her fingers through his, she bathed him in the most beautiful smile he'd ever seen. Full of gratitude and adoration, it was something he wouldn't mind seeing more of.

"Folks might whisper a little when they see you," he warned her while they headed up the front steps.

"Pretty soon, they'll be doing worse than that. I'll have to get used to it sooner or later."

"That's the spirit."

Inside, they walked toward the pew where the family sat every Sunday. In the aisle, Amanda paused and glanced toward the altar. With sunshine streaming in from behind, Daniel Sawyer's famous window looked especially pretty this morning. Or maybe, John mused with a grin, it was because the woman he loved with all his heart was standing beside him. Either way, it was a great start to the day.

"You still see Mary up there?" he asked quietly.

Nodding, Amanda smiled. "I think she's glad to see me."

"I've got no doubt about that."

Pastor Charles hurried into the chapel, looking uncharacteristically flustered until he saw Amanda. Dressed in his customary gray suit and a navy paisley bow tie, he beamed as he turned up the aisle to join them. Reaching out both hands, he shook Amanda's warmly. "Welcome home. It's so wonderful to see you."

"Thank you." As his eyes darted around, she asked, "Is something wrong?"

"Forgive my poor manners, but I just discovered we don't have any teachers for the preschoolers this morning. Some kind of flu is going around, and I'm hunting for a couple of volunteers."

John wasn't keen on a full-time gig in Sunday

school, but he didn't mind helping out occasionally. "I could fill in, if you want."

"Oh, bless you!"

When the pastor looked expectantly at Amanda, she frowned and shook her head. "I haven't been near a church in years. I don't think I'm the kind of person you need."

Understanding warmed his dark eyes, making it clear he wasn't going to question her about why she'd gone astray. "Are you good with crayons and glitter?"

"Emily thinks so."

"For this age group, those are the only qualifications you need. All the materials are in the craft cabinet, and John can introduce you to the kids."

"I don't know." She looked at John, silently asking for his opinion.

Impressed with the pastor's clever strategy for drawing Amanda back into the fold, John figured it was best to keep things light to avoid pressuring her. She'd been through an emotional wringer the last few days, and he didn't want to be guilty of adding to it. "You'd come in handy when the girls need to go to the bathroom."

The minister chuckled. "That sounds settled to me."

"I guess so," Amanda commented, not sounding settled at all.

He thanked them both, giving them each an

approving pat on the shoulder before moving on to greet another family coming through the door.

"Are you nuts?" she hissed at John as they went downstairs. "These kids don't know who I am. What am I going to say to them?"

"Kyle and Emily liked you right off, so do whatever you did that day. Besides, I thought it might be better to start slow before taking on the adults upstairs."

"You nailed that one, Sawyer. I always thought Matt was the smart one."

"He is." Grinning, John opened the door marked *Little Lambs*. He wasn't sure if the label referred to their size or how their usual teacher wanted them to behave. "But even a blind squirrel finds an acorn once in a while."

"There's a lot more of them than there are of us," she muttered in a tone just short of panic.

He chuckled to put her more at ease. "For someone who survived driving on those crazy L.A. freeways, you sure are jumpy."

That got him a decidedly sour face, and for a second he thought she might actually stick her tongue out at him. "You're not helping."

"Call the girls 'sweetie' and the boys 'big guy' or something like that. Then you smile, get 'em a juice box or a tissue, and help with the scissors."

"You make it sound so easy."

"No sense making a problem where there isn't

one. They're kids, you're their pretty substitute teacher." Leaning in, he murmured, "If all else fails, you've got a secret weapon."

"What's that?"

After checking to make sure the kids weren't listening, he discreetly pointed to a locked cabinet marked *Cleaning Supplies.* "That's where they keep the cookies."

Winking, he put a finger to his lips, and she laughed. "*Ooo,* real James Bond kind of stuff."

"When you get in a jam, they're a real lifesaver."

Now that she was in a better frame of mind, he set about showing her just how much fun Sunday school could be. There were ten kids—four boys and six girls—which should be easy enough to manage for an hour. They all chimed in on the short Bible verses they'd learned for today, then sang a very off-key version of "Jesus Loves Me." About five minutes in, Amanda had relaxed enough to smile and enjoy herself.

"You're right," she whispered to him on her way to the art-supply cabinet. "This *is* fun."

"Told ya." A little girl shyly tapped his shoulder, and he turned to her. "Need something?"

"Could you cut this for me?"

"Sure." After doing a quick circuit around a picture of Mary riding a donkey, he handed it back to her. "There ya go."

"Thank you."

Blue eyes sparkling with delight, she gave him a dimpled smile and took back her project. Her cloud of blond curls bounced along as she returned to her friends at a nearby table. She reminded John of Amanda when he'd first met her a lifetime ago, and he wondered if Amanda's daughter would look like that someday.

If things between them went the way they were headed, he just might be around to find out.

"I'm totally amazed," Amanda commented as she sat down next to him. "You're really great with kids."

"Well, they kinda get what I'm about. We have a lot in common."

Resting her chin on her hand, she asked, "Like what?"

"Mostly, we like to have fun." Nudging her shoulder, he got a pretty smile.

"You do it very well. You're going to make a wonderful father someday."

Standing, she gave him a quick peck on the cheek on her way to break up an argument over the rainbow glitter. Blown away by her praise, John stared after her, not sure what to think. No one had ever said anything to him about being a father, much less a good one. He was the footloose, easygoing Sawyer, whose only ties were to the farm he'd loved his entire life.

But his growing feelings for Amanda—and the precious child she was carrying—were making him rethink all that. Sure, he'd taken on more responsibility in the business, but this was different. Deeply personal, and more than a little terrifying, the idea of two people relying on him that way made him wonder.

Was he ready? Would he ever be?

Late one morning, John snuck around the corner of the house to do a little recon. Amanda was on the side porch, singing along with a classic rock station while the washing machine sloshed in the background. Grinning, he trotted back to the kitchen and set his surprise on the table.

Wrapped in silver foil and topped with a multicolored bow that looked like fireworks, he was pretty proud of himself for thinking of it. If Amanda liked it half as much as he thought she would, he was golden.

He poured himself a glass of sweet tea and grabbed a handful of oatmeal cookies, skimming the newspaper while he waited.

When she came through the door with a basket of towels in hand, she greeted him with a smile. "Hey there. How's the haying coming along?"

"Slow without Ridge, but as long as the weather holds we'll be fine." Glancing at the calendar, he couldn't miss the red rings around today's date.

"The doctor said once Marianne got this far, the twins could be born anytime. Have you heard anything yet?"

She shook her head and started folding. "I'm trying to be cool about it so the kids don't get nervous, but I have to tell you, it's driving me nuts."

"Yeah, that's how it was when Caty was close to having Hailey. It's best to keep busy."

"So that works for you?"

"More or less," he confided with a grin.

When she looked directly at him, her eyes landed on the brightly wrapped box. "What's that?"

"I dunno. It was here when I came in."

"Really?" As she crossed the kitchen to join him, her eyes narrowed suspiciously. "Or did you bring it with you?"

"I've got no clue what you're talking about."

"You really need to stick with the truth, Sawyer," she advised with a laugh. "You're a tragically bad liar."

That was the spunky girl he'd fallen in love with before he even knew what it meant. These past few weeks, he'd seen more of her, and less of the frightened mom-to-be he'd comforted outside the clinic. Amanda seemed to be hitting her stride in her new life, and he liked that.

Impatient as ever, she didn't pick at the shiny paper, but tore it open with a vengeance to find out what was inside. When she saw it, she gave him a confused look, then said, "Oh, it's not what the box says."

John couldn't imagine why it mattered, but he corrected her. "No, it's what it says."

"You got me a smartphone?"

Her tone had gone flat and cool, so he couldn't tell if she was surprised or upset. Figuring it was best to cover all his bases, he shrugged. "CPR keeps getting calls here at the farm, which isn't real professional. They were offering a deal, so I added you to my wireless plan when I upgraded."

"You don't have a wireless plan," she pointed out sharply. "You have one of those pay-as-you-go phones."

Grinning, he pulled his fancy new toy out of a cargo pocket in his jeans. "Cool, huh? Caty helped me program it. It's got a camera, and I downloaded the Atlanta Braves app so I can keep up with the team when I'm too busy to watch the games."

"You bought a smartphone. Incredible."

She made it sound like he'd purchased something way beyond him, and his back went up a little. "I'm not a techno-geek, but I'm not totally clueless, either. I know how to do stuff online."

While his temper simmered, he noticed that she hadn't so much as touched her gift. Irked by the whole thing, he asked, "Is there a problem?"

Leaning back in her chair, she seemed to be considering her response carefully. As if he was a child who needed things explained to him very slowly. "John, I really appreciate what you meant to do."

"But?"

Looking him straight in the eyes, she shook her head. "Didn't I tell you I like handling things on my own?"

"Sure, and I told you I'd help you if I could." Nodding at his unappreciated surprise, he went on. "This is me helping."

"No, this is you forcing me to take something I don't want by wrapping it in pretty paper and making it a present. If we'd gone to the store together and you'd asked me if I wanted a phone, I'd have said thank you, but no." Folding her arms, she nailed him with a chiding glare. "You didn't give me the chance, so now I'm the bad guy refusing your generosity."

"It's for your business, so you can talk to clients."

"I can do that from any phone in Harland," she pointed out coolly. "This phone is a completely unnecessary expense—one that I can't afford."

So that was it, John realized. Eager to ease her mind, he waved off her concern. "Don't worry. I'll pay for it."

As soon as the words left his mouth, he knew

he'd made a serious mistake. Ted had dangled a similar offer months ago, promising to take care of her if she'd agree to terminate her pregnancy. Judging by the ice forming in her eyes, she considered John's proposal one step above that one.

Pressing her hands on the table, she stood and glowered at him like something nasty she'd stepped in. The fact that she didn't say anything gave him a pretty good idea how furious she was.

Well, that was fine with him. He was pretty mad himself, and he stood up, too. It worked for Matt, towering over people and looking down at them, so John decided to give it a shot. He needed some kind of edge over this feisty blonde.

Smart as she was, he figured she'd respond best to reason. "You're overreacting. You know that, right?"

Glaring mercilessly, she held her arms out, which pushed her growing stomach into the center of their argument. "Comes with the territory."

"Aw, don't blame the baby. That's not fair."

"Fine. I'll blame you, then. This is the twenty-first century, Sawyer. Women are perfectly capable of managing their own lives without interference from cavemen like you."

As her eyes narrowed to glittering slits, John actually considered backing up a step or two. How did Matt and Ridge navigate such dangerous territory? Maybe there was a map they hadn't told him about.

He'd have to ask them later. For now, he focused on smoothing Amanda's ruffled feathers. "I was only trying to help."

"If I wanted that kind of help, I'd have stayed in California."

Before he could stammer some kind of intelligent response, the phone rang. Turning her back on him, she went to the wall and picked up the handset. "Sawyer Farm." After listening for a few moments, she nodded. "Okay, Ridge. Give Marianne a hug from me and tell her the kids will be there soon."

Their argument forgotten, John bellowed, "Kyle! Emily!"

They came bounding down the stairs, their excited faces making it clear they knew what was up. Grinning, he opened the back door and fished his keys out of his pocket. "Your dad just called to tell us Andrew and Chelsea are on their way. Let's go meet 'em."

When Amanda didn't move to join them, Emily tugged on her hand. "Come on. You're going to help Mommy take care of the new babies, so they have to meet you, too."

Amanda flashed John a panicky look, but he quickly averted his eyes as they headed outside. If she wanted to go with them, fine. If not, that was fine, too. Infuriatingly headstrong and sharper than she needed to be, she drove him completely over the edge sometimes. He recalled Matt complaining about those same qualities in his sassy wife. More than once.

Maybe, John thought as he dialed Matt's number on his fancy new phone, that was part of their charm.

"Hey, Matt. Ridge called, and we're on our way to the hospital with the kids. My car's full, so you should pick up your girls and meet us there." Setting the speakerphone the way Caty had showed him, he checked the kids' seat belts and started his Triumph while Matt growled about finishing this round of haying. "Stay out there by yourself, I don't care. I'm gonna go see my new niece and nephew."

Matt was in midrant when John clicked off the phone. Matt's Led Zeppelin ringtone went off almost immediately, and it actually sounded angry. John pressed the decline button and turned onto the highway that led to Kenwood.

"Boy, are you gonna be in trouble," Kyle warned. "Uncle Matt hates it when you ignore him like that."

Too excited to worry about riling his big brother's notorious temper, John grinned into the rearview mirror. "Kid, I've been doing it all my life."

"True," Amanda agreed, "and it always made him furious."

Deciding to test the waters, John joked, "Everyone's good at something."

When she didn't respond, he slanted a glance over to find her staring out at the fields whipping by. Not ready to make nice, he thought with a mental sigh. *Stubborn* wasn't the word for her sometimes.

"Amanda, how long have you and Uncle John known each other?" Emily asked.

"I was four when my family moved here. Your uncle and I met in Sunday school and started arguing about who should get the grape-colored crayon."

That she remembered a tiny detail like that did something funky to John's heart. They had so much history together, and now she was back in his life. Like a wrecking ball, knocking down all the defenses he'd built so he wouldn't have to take anything too seriously. Much as he'd like to reclaim the carefree attitude he'd cultivated all these years, those days were gone.

It had taken him a long time to realize he loved Amanda Gardner. Now that he had, he couldn't imagine his days without her.

Keeping his eyes on the road, he found her hand on the center console and gave it a little squeeze. When she laced her fingers through his, the knot that had been tightening his chest started to unravel, and he found himself breathing more easily.

Later, they could talk about his well-intentioned but clumsy attempt to be helpful. She'd scold him for being overbearing, he'd apologize for not respecting her need to be self-sufficient. She could keep the phone or not, whichever she preferred. All he wanted was for her to smile up at him and tell him she loved him.

And if she wanted to end their fight with a kiss, he wouldn't complain.

Chapter Eleven

Amanda could feel John tense up the instant they set foot inside the lobby of Kenwood Community Hospital. The excitement he'd been projecting faded noticeably, and she couldn't miss his long look at the sign that showed visitors the way to the ICU. She could only imagine what was going through his head, and she slid an arm around him in support.

Grimacing, he murmured, "I hate this place. Mom died here, and we never got to say goodbye."

"Hailey was also born here," she reminded him firmly. "And now Andrew and Chelsea are coming into the world, so that means the good will outweigh the bad."

After a few moments, he gave her a half smile and dropped a kiss on top of her head. "Yeah, I guess you're right. Thanks."

"Anytime."

The kids had stopped in front of the gift shop window and were quarreling about something that had snagged their attention.

"What's up, guys?" she asked as she and John paused behind them.

"Emily wants to get the babies something." Kyle pointed at a cluster of stuffed animals. "I told her they can't have stuff like that 'til they're older."

"I still think Chelsea would like the bunny and Andrew would like that turtle," Emily protested.

"Drew," Kyle corrected her. "We're calling him Drew."

"I still think he'd like it," she went on as if he hadn't scolded her. "It's really cute."

The girl's thoughtfulness was touching, and Amanda nodded. "They are. You know, we could buy them now and keep them on a shelf in the nursery until the twins are old enough to play with them."

Kyle nodded. "That works. But we didn't bring any money."

"Guess you'll have to work 'em off, then," John teased. "You two head in and start your shift. We'll pick you up on the way out."

Hands on her hips, Emily glared up at him as if he didn't loom over her like a massive tree over a sapling. "Uncle John, that is so not funny."

He made a uniquely male sound that was half groan and half laugh. "Oh, man. You sound just like your Aunt Lisa."

Her glare mellowed into the most adorable smile on the planet. "What a nice thing to say. Thank you."

"You're welcome."

Grumbling, John took out his wallet to pay for the gifts. Once they were back on track, Kyle navigated the way to the maternity waiting area. The place was full of toys, right down to a small plastic playground set and two TVs connected to video-game consoles. Delighted, the kids ditched Amanda and John and started making friends.

As they approached the seating area, Amanda pulled him to a stop and gave him a quick kiss. "Love you, Sawyer."

Settling his arms around her, he gave her the smile that could melt the iciest heart in North Carolina. "Love you, too, Gardner. Do I need to apologize?"

"For being so generous you want to help me get my business up and running?" Despite her earlier aggravation, she shook her head. "It's me who should apologize. This is totally different than my situation in California, and I don't know why I reacted that way. I feel terrible."

"So you'll keep the phone?" he asked with a hopeful expression. "I mean, it would be good to have one while you're out, just in case you need something."

Now it was starting to make sense. He was concerned about her not being able to call someone if she was in trouble. Determined to maintain her precious independence, she'd done the equivalent of kicking a puppy who wanted nothing more than to love her. "Is that where this is coming from? You're worried about me?"

"Well, you're out with the kids a lot, and if something happens, you should have a phone."

"Not that nice a phone."

He shrugged as if the cost wasn't a big deal to him. "You can have whatever kind you want. As long as I'm on the speed dial, I don't care."

All those years in L.A. had jaded her, Amanda realized. She'd learned to examine people's behavior for ulterior motives, not take them at face value. Ted's heartless proposal had driven the lesson home, and she'd transferred her cynical view of the world to John.

Only, John was the least manipulative person she'd ever met. He wasn't perfect, but he was the kind of guy who said what he meant and meant what he said. Fortunately for her, one of his faults was that he had a weakness for mouthy blondes.

"Which number on the speed dial?" she asked as they found a love seat within view of the play area and sat down.

Stretching his arms across the back of the sofa, he crossed his long legs in front of him and nearly blinded her with his aw-shucks country-boy grin. "Number one, of course."

"Of course," she retorted primly, yanking his chain a little. Despite their earlier misunderstanding, she really enjoyed sparring with him, knowing he'd give it right back to her, no hard feelings. "You certainly think a lot of yourself."

That got her a shameless grin. "No reason not to."

She was just about to zing him for being conceited when a sudden sharp pain in her back put an end to the fun. Reaching behind her, she discovered she couldn't reach it. Before she could even ask, John unfolded himself from his lazy pose and moved his hand in circles over her lower back until she hummed. "Right there."

Gently as first, then more firmly, he massaged the muscle until the knot was finally gone. Sighing in relief, she carefully leaned against him to avoid another spasm. "Thank you."

"Anytime."

As his arm tightened around her in a half hug, she closed her eyes and tried to relax. She'd just begun to doze off when Kyle yelled, "Dad!"

"Hey, you guys." Still dressed in blue scrubs and booties, Ridge's grin was so huge, it was threatening to crack his face wide open. "Marianne's not ready for company yet, but I thought you might like to see some pictures."

The kids crowded in, and he thumbed across the screen on his phone. "Nope, not that one. Your mom would kill me. Here's a good one."

Leaning closer, they all *ooed* and *ahhed* over the two wrinkly but healthy babies.

"Which one is Chelsea?" Emily wanted to know. When Ridge pointed her out, the little girl smiled. "She's really pretty, isn't she, Daddy?"

"She looks just like you, sweetness."

"Drew's bigger, though," Kyle said. "That's good, 'cause us Sawyer boys have to be big and strong. Right, Uncle John?"

"Got that right. We'll have him out on a tractor in no time."

"Or up in a plane crop dusting," Ridge suggested. "I'd like to think there's a little of me in there, too."

The comment had apparently slipped out without his thinking about it, because he stared at the picture frozen on the screen and smiled. While Amanda had seen for herself how much he adored Kyle and Emily, there was obviously something different about actually being his children's father.

Would John feel the same way? She didn't doubt for a second that he could love her daughter, but even if he adopted her, there would always be something missing. That unbreakable Sawyer bond wouldn't be part of the equation, no matter what he did.

The realization made her want to cry, so she firmly pushed it away. Today was for celebrating Drew and Chelsea coming into the world, not dreading the birth of a child with no family to call her own.

"Come on, Chelsea," Amanda pleaded in a whisper, bouncing the fussy three-week-old in a slightly different way. She'd fled to the back porch, hoping to keep the house quiet enough for everyone else to remain asleep. "Your mama needs some sleep, so I'm it. Work with me here."

That got her a few precious seconds of silence, and she began to relax. Big mistake. Once she loosened her hold, the baby started up again. Amanda hadn't thought she could get any louder, but she'd been wrong. She couldn't have been wronger.

Was that even a word? she wondered, realizing she was punchy from a severe lack of sleep. Marianne was still a few days away from being allowed on her feet, so a lot of the fetching and carrying of infants had fallen to Amanda, Ridge and John. None of them was getting much rest, but they'd all agreed to a rotating baby-care schedule to allow Marianne time to recuperate.

Right now, Amanda was regretting taking Ridge's shift.

No good deed goes unpunished.

In her memory, she could hear her father reciting one of his personal philosophies. A pessimist to the core, he always saw the darkest side of any situation. Puppies made messes. Kids made too much noise. Once, when she'd pointed out a rainbow near their home, he'd muttered about the rain washing out his round of golf.

She didn't want to be that way, Amanda thought as she cradled Chelsea in her other arm. She wanted to see the bright, positive angles in life, no matter how bad things got. The way John did.

As if on cue, she heard his front screen door creak open and slam shut. Tucker zoomed in from wherever he'd been and took off down the lane. A few seconds later, she saw the two of them making their way toward the main house.

A huge yawn split John's handsome face, and he dragged his fingers through still-damp hair. It was four in the morning, and with harvest season nearly over, she knew he'd be out in the fields by five. He normally started his day by rolling out of bed and pulling on whatever clothes were handy. Even allowing for a shower, he could have snuck in another half hour of sleep. That he'd given that up and was coming to help her out brought a rush of tears to her eyes.

"Hey now." He hurried to join her on the porch. "What's wrong?"

"Nothing. It's just that Chelsea won't calm down, and I really have to go to the bathroom."

"Clean and fed?" he asked.

"Of course. I'm not an idiot." She heard the snap in her tone and took a deep breath. "Sorry. There's a loose shutter outside my window, and it banged all night. I didn't get much sleep, and then I was up with the babies."

"I'll fix it this afternoon."

"You're so busy…"

"What? I don't have five minutes and a hammer?"

The tension she'd been fighting eased a little, and she managed a smile. "Thanks."

"No problem." Holding out his hands, he carefully lifted Chelsea and settled her against his chest. Instantly, she stopped crying and cuddled in like a perfectly well-behaved child.

"Show-off."

"We all have our talents."

"I think you have more than the legal limit," Amanda accused as she headed inside.

Behind her, he chuckled quietly, and she had to smile. Maddening as he could be, John Sawyer was by far the best guy she'd ever known. Much as she treasured her independence, she honestly didn't know what she'd do without him.

Once Chelsea fell asleep, John figured the best thing was not to mess with whatever he'd done that had gotten her that way. So he settled into the white wicker rocker on the back porch and chatted with Amanda through the screen.

"How's business?" he asked while she got the coffee going.

"Better. I picked up another client this week, so that makes four. Ruthy's the best advertising I could have asked for." Batter bowl in hand, she came to the back door. Barefoot, she was wearing a flowery dress with a belt that tied above her waist. The pale colors highlighted her eyes, and she was finally glowing the way pregnant women were supposed to.

"That's a pretty dress."

"Marianne insisted on giving it to me. She said she got big so fast, she never got a chance to wear it, so it still had the tag on it." John tried not to smile, but when she pinned him with a knowing look, he knew he hadn't quite managed it. "Lisa bought this for me, and they made up that story so I wouldn't get mad."

"I'm not sayin' nothin'."

She rolled her eyes, but let the subject drop. "Whatever. I forgot to tell you—Ruthy's got a room coming open at the beginning of October, and she promised to hold it for me. That's when Marianne wants to move the twins into their nursery, so the timing is perfect for me to move into town."

John's heart plunged to the weathered floorboards, and it was all he could do to hold still and avoid awakening his niece. All this time, he'd known Amanda would be leaving at some point. But now that there was a timetable attached to her plans, he didn't know how to take it. "Sounds good."

Apparently, his reaction didn't come across as casually as he'd intended. Setting the bowl down, she opened the door and settled on the footrest in front of him. "John, I can't stay here. Now that we're together, folks are starting to talk."

"So? It's not like you're spending the night at my place or anything."

"Try to understand." Resting a hand on his arm, her expression begged him to be reasonable. "I've got enough strikes against me, being pregnant and single. I know God's forgiven me, but people are harder. If they think I'm still making the same mistakes, they won't be able to look past them to all the good things I'm trying to do."

"I don't care about that." Reaching out with his free hand, he cradled her cheek in his palm. "I just don't want you to go."

Tilting her head, she gave him a sympathetic look. "I know, and I love you for feeling that way. But I want to do this, because I know it's for the best. I'm sorry you don't like it, but I'm hoping you'll back me up."

"You don't have a car. How are you gonna get around to grocery shop and meet clients and stuff?"

He almost suggested he loan her the money to buy one, but after the phone incident, he'd pulled way back on offering anything beyond help with chores. She was using the phone, though stubbornly insisting on paying her portion of the bill every month. Either that, she'd told him, or she would return it to the store. Faced with that choice, he'd reluctantly accepted the compromise.

Of course, the invoice came to him at the farm. He wasn't the most organized person, so he had all his bills on autopay and never gave them a second thought. It wouldn't be his fault if he forgot to mention it to her.

"Ruthy said she's never in her office during the day, so I can use it when I have meetings. I can walk to that little market on Main Street, and they have everything I'll need."

"Once the baby comes, you'll have to take her to the doctor."

"There's a shuttle into Kenwood a few times a day," she replied. "I'll use that."

"Staying at Ruthy's is supposed to be temporary. You can't live there forever."

"I know, but once I have some money, I can start rebuilding my credit. Then I can get an apartment and a used car, and things will improve from there." Leaning in, she gave him a long kiss. "When I came home, I felt like I was crawling along the ground, just trying to get back on my feet again. I know now that God brought me back here because this was where I needed to be. You helped me stand on my own two feet, and your family gave me a chance to pull my life back together. No matter where I'm living, I will never, ever forget that."

He'd have to be content with that, he realized. Amanda had already made the decision, and she'd made it for the right reasons. He didn't have much choice but to go along. "You know I love you, right?"

Bathing him in a grateful smile, she nodded. "I love you, too. More than anything in the world."

"And I can come visit?"

"I'd be mad if you didn't." After a pause, she added, "When I'm waddling around like a penguin, it would be nice not to have to ride the shuttle. I could use a ride to the doctor once in a while, if you have time."

For you? Always.

The sentiment nearly escaped before he could

catch it. He didn't want to ruin her excitement by having her think he was suddenly getting all mushy. She was moving a few miles away, he reminded himself, and he could make that trip in five minutes. Four if there was something important on the other end. He couldn't imagine anything ever being more important to him than Amanda, but the sun had barely poked through, and he'd had his fill of serious conversation.

"Just hit number one on your speed dial," he said with a grin. "I'll be there."

Chapter Twelve

John had been dreading this day.

It was the beginning of October, and Ruthy's spare room was ready for Amanda. He'd tried a few more times to convince her to stay at the farm, but, as usual, once she made up her mind, it was set in stone.

Matt had warned him about smart women, John reminded himself as he trudged up the diner's back stairs, carrying a box of bedding and towels. He should have listened. Then again, he'd dated plenty of sweet, obliging women who cheerfully went along with whatever he said. None of them fascinated him the way Amanda did.

He was hopeless.

"Okay, lady." He faked a Brooklyn accent as he strolled through the open door. "Where d'ya want dese?"

Amanda laughed. "Why are you talking like that?"

Dropping his load, John turned to Seth. "See what I have to put up with?"

"Don't drag me into this. I'm busy." After getting an approving peck on the cheek from his wife, Seth tossed John a quick, sympathetic look and got back to work.

He was holding up a framed painting of a quaint English cottage, moving it along the wall while Lisa tilted her head this way and that. "Right there. Amanda, what do you think?"

"Perfect. I'll feel like I'm eating my meals at a sidewalk café in London. I can't believe you two made that for me."

"When you said last month how much you love London, I decided to make this my next project," Lisa told her with a warm smile. "Fortunately, my hubby can make a custom frame in his sleep."

He chuckled. "As fast as you paint, I get a lot of practice."

Marianne was busy stocking the cupboards, while Caty filled the fridge. Meanwhile, Matt was loosening up the single window so it would open, and Ridge was making sure Amanda's laptop could hook into Ruthy's wireless internet connection. Kyle and Emily had the younger kids corralled in the tiny bathroom, entertaining them while their parents got Amanda's things squared away.

The small apartment was filled to bursting, and

there wasn't all that much left to do. John noticed the box he'd brought up still on the floor, so he grabbed the fitted sheet and started making the single bed.

"Wait," Amanda teased, hugging him from behind. "Let me get my camera."

He flung the top sheet out and started tucking the corners in. "What? I know how to make a bed."

"Not your own."

"Nobody cares about that."

"I do," Marianne pointed out as she opened the bathroom door to collect her crew. "But you never listen to me. Everything's put away, so we'll be going. Kids, let's say goodbye to Amanda and let her get settled."

The official order was for the under-twenty crowd, but everyone else got the drift and took off after a quick round of hugs. That left John alone with Amanda, something he'd been both hoping for and wanting to avoid.

They'd talked several times about her moving out, and he'd finally come to terms with it. At least, that's what he kept telling himself. When he picked up a pillow and a faded pillowcase, she grasped his hands to stop them.

"Have I thanked you?" she asked quietly.

Not wanting to dim her enthusiasm, he grinned at her. "Not today."

Bathing him in the most beautiful of her many smiles, she stood on tiptoe and kissed him. He brought her as close as he could, wishing he never had to let her go. Nosing aside the soft cloud of curls by her ear, he murmured, "I'm gonna miss you, Gardner."

"I'm gonna miss you, too, Sawyer. Every day." *Please come home with me.*

He came dangerously close to saying those words out loud before reason kicked in and stopped him. Even if she wanted to stay at the farm, their guest room was now the nursery, and there was nowhere for her to sleep. Once her baby arrived, they'd need their own place, and for now this was it.

Reluctantly, he let her go and stepped back, keeping her circled in his arms. "You've got everything?"

Glancing around, she giggled. "I hope so. There's no room for anything else."

He appreciated her trying to make this easier for him, but for once he was serious. "Call me anytime you need something."

With a flirty grin, she toyed with the fraying collar of his flannel shirt. "What if I just need to see you?"

She was rarely the more lighthearted of the two of them, and he joined in with a grin. "I'll be here in four minutes."

Leaning in, he gave her one last kiss and headed for the door. Pausing there, he looked back at her and did his best to smile. "See ya."

As he dragged his feet into the hallway and down the stairs, John knew she was safe, and that this was what she wanted. But walking away from her was the hardest thing he'd ever done in his life.

"People are staring," Amanda complained as she and John strolled out of Carolina Collectibles one evening. The air was crisp, with the scent of dry leaves and wood smoke floating on the breeze. While they walked along Main Street, the half moon glowed overhead, stars twinkling like sparklers in the sky.

"It's the bear." Grinning over at her, he adjusted the humongous brown teddy bear he was carrying piggyback style.

The pink gingham bow around its neck was just too much, and she smiled. "Hailey's going to love that. I'm not sure about Matt, though."

"He'll hate it," John predicted confidently. "That's half the fun."

She was in midlaugh when she caught a glimpse of herself in a dark store window. She was wearing the flowery dress John liked, but she hadn't seen it full length in a while. Angling for a side view, she groaned. "I don't really look like that, do I?"

"Since you've been in sweats and huge T-shirts lately, I wouldn't know."

Even those were getting tight, Amanda thought with a grimace. She'd seen the pictures, both at the doctor's office and in her book. Intellectually, she understood that when you were carrying another person around in your body, things had to expand to accommodate the baby. Seeing it on herself was something else again.

"This is so not how things were supposed to be," she groused, seething at the unfairness of life in general. "I went to a great college, got my MBA and was supposed to have my own fabulously successful PR firm by the time I was forty. Instead, I have this."

Flinging her arms out, she ended her hissy fit with a nice dramatic flair. The entire time, she was painfully aware that she was making a complete fool of herself.

Plunking the bear on a nearby bench, John sat and patted the open space beside him. "Okay, Gardner. What's really bothering you?"

Crossing her arms over her stomach, she shot him a nasty look. "How do you know that's not it?"

The moron didn't even blink. Spreading his arms out the way he always did when he sat still for more than ten seconds, he waited. He didn't speak, but the twinkle in his eyes told her he'd sit there all night if that was what it took.

While Amanda wasn't keen on having personal conversations in such a public space, she was so irritated she broke her own rule. Sitting down, she tried to frame her thoughts so she wouldn't come off sounding like a total harpy. "I appreciate everyone's help—really I do."

"But you want to do things your own way. Drive yourself around, use your own computer." He toyed with the fluttery skirt of her dress. "Wear your own clothes."

"Exactly. I'm used to being independent, and being so much the opposite is driving me crazy." Now that she'd voiced her frustration, all the fight went out of her, and she suddenly felt exhausted. Resting her cheek on his shoulder, she heaved a pathetic sound that fell somewhere between a sigh and a sob. "Sometimes I just want my old life back. I'd be smarter this time around."

"Life changes as we go along," he reminded her, dropping a kiss on her temple. "But you and little Sophie or Karen or whoever won't have to do everything on your own."

Angling her head, she gave him a grateful smile. "I'll have you."

"And babysitters and teachers. Hopefully, your

ents will change their minds and decide they want to get to know their grandbaby."

When she moaned, he didn't scold her for being hardheaded. "I know you like to be in control of everything, but it doesn't always work that way. You have to take what God's given you and do the best you can with it."

"I don't want to." Knowing she sounded like a spoiled brat, she added, "But I will because I have to."

"He'll help you through this, if you let Him." Curling his arm around her, John rested his chin on her head. "And so will I."

Tears welled up in her eyes, and she burrowed closer to this wonderful, aggravating man who had offered her so much, asking for nothing in return. John believed she was worthy of his love, and she'd gradually come to believe it herself. The realization humbled her, and she sent up a silent prayer.

Thank you, God, for bringing us together.

"I got an email from Ted's wife today," she ventured, hoping John would take it well.

"Really? Isn't that kinda weird?"

"Very, but she found my address in Ted's computer and thought I'd like to know she's divorcing him. Apparently she's in the process of taking him to the cleaner's."

"Ouch."

"Most of their money was hers, so it's only fair."

"Speaking of money, any word on that slimy accountant of yours?"

"Not a peep. I guess he's disappeared into some jungle somewhere. It doesn't matter anyway," she added, hugging John's arm. "My life is much better now."

"You mean you don't miss your Porsche and living on the beach and all those fancy restaurants you used to eat at?"

"The only things I miss are lattes and yoga. I think I've talked Ruthy into putting in an espresso machine, and when I can see my feet again, I'll find some DVDs and get back in shape."

Chuckling, John kissed the top of her head. "So after all these years, you finally figured out Harland's not as bad as you thought."

"Don't gloat, Sawyer. It's not nice."

While they sat in comfortable silence, one by one the bells from each of the four churches began tolling eight. Shifting a little, John uncrossed his legs. "If you don't want folks seeing me at your place too late, we should get back."

"Eight o'clock counts as late," she commented as he got up and helped her to her feet. "This town is too much."

"You're the one who wants people to think you're all grown-up and respectable." He slung the bear over his shoulders again. "Me? I couldn't care less."

"So you've said. Many times."

As they approached Ruthy's Place, Amanda noticed there were a lot more lights on than usual. "Hmm—let me guess. This little shopping trip was a ruse to get me out of my apartment so Caty and your sisters could set up a baby shower."

"And Ruthy and Priscilla Fairman, and most of the Harland Ladies' League," John added. "They're always up for a party."

"That's quite a guest list. And now I'm thinking this bear isn't really for Hailey."

"Busted," he confessed with a grin.

"You're very sweet, but I'm not sure I have room for it."

"It'll fit in the windowsill. I measured."

"You did?" The fact that he'd thought ahead for her daughter's gift touched her deeply. Standing on tiptoe, she gave him a quick kiss. "Love you, Sawyer."

"Back at ya, Gardner."

Returning the kiss, he pulled open the door and stepped back so she had the spotlight all to herself.

As Caty and John's sisters rushed over to greet her, Amanda had to remind herself she was actually in Ruthy's diner. Everywhere she looked, there was something pink, white or frilly. The bistro tables and chairs that normally sat out front were in a cozy section of the dining room, with vases of wildflowers in the center of each table. On the lunch counter sat a huge bowl filled with ribbons, note cards and clothespins. Next to it was a stack of small paper bags—apparently the traditional shower games.

After she'd taken it all in, she still couldn't believe they'd gone to so much trouble. Considering her circumstances, she was touched by the effort they'd all put in to make her feel special. "This is amazing, guys. You didn't have to do all this just for me."

"Just for you," Ruthy clucked as she pulled Amanda into a hug. "We do this for everyone when they're expecting, don't we girls?"

"Any excuse for a party," the woman mixing up punch agreed.

Several others echoed the comment, and Amanda couldn't help noticing how excited everyone looked. To top it off, Danielle Benton appeared from the kitchen, carrying the biggest cake Amanda had ever seen. Decorated with icing flowers in every shade of pink imaginable, it looked like the bouquet from a wedding.

"I hope you don't mind, Amanda," she said as

she set the beautiful cake on a table draped with lace tablecloths. "This is my shower gift."

Amanda laughed. "Mind? It's gorgeous. I'm just sorry we have to cut it into pieces."

"Pictures first!" Lisa insisted, holding up her camera.

"On that note," John said, chuckling, "I'd better go."

"Whatsa matter, big guy?" Lisa teased. "Afraid the pink will rub off on you?"

Grinning, he backpedaled toward the door. "Something like that. Enjoy your evening, ladies."

When he turned and left the diner, Amanda heard a few murmured compliments on the view.

Eat your heart out, girls, she thought with a grin. *He's mine.*

On a chilly day in early November, Amanda found herself at a dead end.

Sitting at the kitchen table in her tiny studio apartment, she stared at the painting Seth and Lisa had given her, searching the quaint setting for inspiration. She was trying to generate some catchy slogans for her latest client, a pet-sitting service. So far, the best she'd come up with was "Enjoy your time away while…"

Over the years, she'd learned plenty of tricks for unblocking your creative mind, but no matter what she tried, the opening was as far as she got.

The concept was not to worry while you're gone, because this devoted animal lover will make sure your pets are well cared-for in your absence. On time, any species, reasonable rates.

Those were her notes, but the more she read through them, the more the words started to blur together. Realizing that she'd hit a wall, she stood and arched her sore back while she walked over to the window.

Waddled, she corrected herself. With only three weeks left to her due date, the penguin gait had taken over, big-time. She slept half-sitting up because getting out of bed had gotten to be so difficult, she was afraid one morning she wouldn't be able to do it and would have to call for a crane. It felt as if her entire life was spinning out of control, at the mercy of the demanding little person growing inside her.

No. Putting a stop to the negative train of thought, she closed her eyes and tipped her head down in silent prayer.

Please, God. Help me through this.

She'd discovered that when she let go of the reins and trusted Him to take care of things, she always felt better. That was the lesson, she realized. It explained why people who leaned on their faith weathered difficult times better than others. They could turn to Someone who had the ultimate wisdom and strength no human being could match. It was comforting, and more than once she'd kicked herself for straying so far away.

But right now, she needed ideas. Harland's streets weren't as bustling as a city's, but there was usually something going on. She would have gone down to mingle, but the stairs were getting tougher to navigate with the extra weight she was carrying. The trip down was okay, but the daunting prospect of coming back up convinced her to stay put. Pushing aside her longing to join the world, she contented herself with opening the window for some fresh air.

A teenage girl was just leaving the beauty shop, pulling straight, stylishly angled hair over her shoulders before snapping a picture of herself with her phone. Wearing a delighted smile, she tapped away on the screen, obviously sending the photo to someone. Beyond her, two old farmers in jeans and plaid jackets were yacking. One of them slapped the other on the back, and they both laughed loudly enough that she could hear them from her perch two stories up.

She could see quite a bit of the town, and she kept skimming, trolling for PR ideas. As her eyes cruised past the square, they landed on something she would have barely noticed a few months ago. Now, it drew her attention like a magnet.

A young couple was walking with a small child between them. Dressed in overalls and a ball cap, his little sneakers wobbled along as he held both his parents' hands. Clearly learning how to walk, he stopped a few times, and finally plopped down on the sidewalk.

Unfazed, his father scooped him up and tossed him in the air, and he responded with that delighted child's laugh that could make even a heartless miser smile. Then the young father set him down, held him until he was steady, and both parents took the boy's hands again. Headed for the town playground, they tottered along until they were out of her sight.

Every child should have that, she thought as her view swam with tears. A mommy and a daddy, one for each hand, ready to pick her up when she fell and push her on the swings. Her daughter would have only Amanda, who needed to work to support them both.

John was serious about loving her—that much she knew. And she felt the same about him, but they hadn't gotten anywhere near discussing the *M* word yet. While the thought of being someone's wife terrified her, the possibility of divorcing her best friend absolutely paralyzed her. She had no intention of signing on for anything she wasn't confident about, so marriage—if it ever came—could be months or even years away.

That meant she was on her own.

The baby chose that precise moment to go into

her imitation of a mini-Rockette, and Amanda rubbed a hand over the ruckus, hoping to soothe it while she calmed her own nerves. The child refused to settle, and she began to wonder if her daughter was trying to tell her something. Like, "Please, Mommy, give me a real family."

"I can't," Amanda said out loud, feeling horrible. "It won't be that way for us."

All of a sudden, the kicking stopped, and she felt the baby roll in her confined space and stop moving. Amanda knew it was insane, but she felt as if her child had turned away, too disappointed to play with her anymore.

Sobbing uncontrollably, Amanda collapsed into a worn armchair and cried for longer than she ever had in her life. A creative thinker by nature, she firmly believed every problem had a solution. But this time, she was at a loss. While she wallowed in misery of her own making, a commercial came on the radio about foster parents.

"You don't need to be perfect," the kind woman's voice assured her listeners. "You just need to be there."

Nice thought, she mused, but it didn't make her feel any better. After a couple of songs, the message from the ad got through, and she had an epiphany. Maybe, she thought excitedly as she shuffled over to her computer, there was a way.

* * *

Sometimes, rain was a good thing.

They'd kept an eye on the weather all morning, baling their last cutting of hay like there was no tomorrow. Running it straight to the distributor in Kenwood took time, but in the end it meant they only had to load and unload the trucks once. John was on his way back with the last one, empty except for a layer of stray pieces he'd sweep out later.

Right now, he was on his way to surprise Amanda. It was a little early for supper, but she was always hungry these days, so he figured she wouldn't complain. She might even let him pick up the whole tab this time.

He pulled into two open spots that wouldn't clog up the parking in front of anyone's store, then grabbed two white takeout bags from a new chicken place he'd come across on his drive back into town. Dodging raindrops, he got out of the truck and climbed the outside stairs that led to the second-floor landing.

Outside her door, he kicked quietly with his boot. "Room service!"

"John?"

"Yes, ma'am. I have chicken." It took her a few seconds, but he waited patiently, grinning when she opened the door. "It's raining."

When she laughed, it occurred to him that he

hadn't heard that from her much lately. He wondered what had happened to brighten her mood on such a gloomy afternoon.

"I can see that. Come on in." She moved back to let him in and closed the door. Sniffing the air, she smiled. "Smells good."

"Fried for me, broiled for you. How you can eat such bland food is beyond me."

"Less fat equals less to lose after the baby's born."

Being a farmer, John didn't worry much about working off what he ate. "Must be a California thing."

"We aren't all born buff like you. Have a seat, and I'll get some plates."

John plunked himself down in one of the two chairs at her table and noticed her computer open. "Working on that pet-sitting thing?"

"Not exactly."

Her tone should have been all the warning he needed, but he couldn't resist leaning in to see what was on the screen. She hadn't told him not to, but when he read the title, he really wished she had.

His heart lurched into his throat, and he waited a few beats so he'd sound reasonably interested instead of panicked. After all, he didn't know much about PR. Maybe he'd misunderstood. "What are you doing on an adoption website?"

"I'm just getting some information right now." Moving the offensive laptop to the counter, she began setting two places at the table. "Infants are really in demand these days."

"Yeah, so are soybeans," he shot back. Her casual manner irritated him, and he figured the time for being calm had passed. "I can't believe you're thinking about giving away the baby you claim to love so much. Your *daughter*."

Hoping to shame her into seeing reason, he leaned heavily on the last word. She didn't even blink.

"I'm considering this because I do love her so much," Amanda said quietly. "I want her to have everything, and she won't get that with me."

"Everything like what?"

"A mother and father, for starters."

"Give me a break." Growing more frustrated by the second, he reminded her, "Dad raised four kids on his own, and he did a great job."

"I'm not Ethan."

"I know that, but—"

"I'm not discussing this with you anymore," she announced in that high-and-mighty tone he despised. "You've made your feelings clear, but in the end this is my decision."

Slumping in his chair, John picked at the chicken he couldn't wait to rip into five minutes ago. A thought popped into his head, and he pegged Amanda with a very direct look. "Is this why you haven't picked out a name for her? Were you planning to give her away all along?"

"Don't say it like that," Amanda snapped. "I haven't decided anything yet, I'm just exploring the options."

"Your options. She doesn't get a say, does she? 'Cause she's a helpless little baby."

John knew he'd landed a blow when tears started pooling in Amanda's eyes.

"Don't do that to me," she whispered. "This is really, really hard."

It took every ounce of strength he had not to wrap his arms around her and pull her close. But he'd learned that when she needed that, she'd come to him. He did uncross his arms and fold his hands in his lap to give a more open-minded appearance. "You haven't said a word about any of this before. What happened?"

She told him about the little boy and his parents, how idyllic that scene was. "I just want her to have a family like that."

Inspired, John did the most impulsive thing he'd done in his whole impulsive life. "Then let's give her one."

"What?"

Realizing that she wasn't following along, he took her hands in his and went down on one muddy knee beside her. "Amanda, I love you. Will you marry me?"

Gasping, she jerked her hands away, shaking her head so violently, he was afraid she'd snap her neck. She was struggling to get out of her chair, and John felt compelled to help her up. When he tried, she slapped his hand away and pushed herself to her feet. She skittered as far away from him as she could in the small room, and the tears streaming down her face almost did him in.

With his heart tumbling in a free-fall, he gave her the space she was so frantically trying to put between them. Recalling that Amanda cried at puppy-food commercials these days, he went with some humor to lighten the moment. "Did I do that wrong?"

Making a sound that was half sob and half laugh, she shook her head but still refused to meet his eyes. After a few deep breaths, she wiped her cheeks and squared her shoulders before facing him.

"John, that's the sweetest thing anyone's ever said to me. I'm sorry I reacted so badly."

"That's okay." Relief started flooding in, and he felt his heart recovering some altitude.

Her next look sent it spiraling back down again. "But I could never accept your proposal now. It's because of the baby, and I don't want you to regret it."

"I wouldn't." He stood and moved closer, just enough to remind her that he'd promised to be there for her, no matter what. "You've seen me. I love kids, and they're pretty fond of me, too."

"I know." She sounded so miserable, he knew he hadn't quite convinced her. "But this is the rest of our lives you're talking about. You can't just jump off a cliff like that when you don't know what you're getting into."

"It'll be fine. I'm good at winging things."

Wrong choice of words, he realized when she slowly shook her head. "You don't 'wing things'—" she did those annoying air quotes "—when a child is involved. I have a few weeks still, and I'll make a rational, mature decision about what to do. I hope you'll agree with it."

"And if I don't?"

She arched one eyebrow, looking so calm her meaning was crystal clear. If he didn't go along, it didn't matter. Amanda was doing what she wanted, just as she always did.

After all they'd been through, the massive effort he'd put in to make her feel safe and loved, nothing had changed.

"I just need for you to understand," she confessed, easing back a touch.

Oddly enough, her emotional appeal was what finally set him off.

Furious, he pointed to the laptop screen, still

frozen on the adoption website. "I'll never understand how you could even *think* of giving your baby away." When she opened her mouth to protest, he cut her off. "Don't correct me, 'cause that's what it is. You're perfectly capable of giving your daughter the family you want her to have, but you won't because you're too scared and stubborn to marry me."

"Even if it was just you and me, I would've said no. It's a huge step, and I don't want either of us committing to it until we're absolutely sure it's going to work."

"You want a family—I offered you one."

"You're not ready for that right now, and you know it. You only asked so I'll keep the baby."

Her phrasing had taken on a more positive note, and John felt a glimmer of hope flare inside him. "Will you?"

In reply, she frowned and bit her lip. He could see she was confused, but she'd taken a stand and refused to back away from it. "Quit badgering me and let me figure this out for myself."

Outmaneuvered by a gorgeous blonde with an exasperating mind of her own, John finally admitted defeat.

"Fine." Fishing the keys out of his pocket, he headed for the door. There was a good chance they'd never discuss this again, so he thought it best to make his position absolutely clear. Turning, he looked her dead in the eyes.

"But if you give this child away, we're done. You might as well go back to California and never come back."

With that, he spun on his heel and stalked out, slamming the door behind him.

Chapter Thirteen

It was the Friday before Thanksgiving, and the Sawyers had gathered for their customary family supper. Something was up this week, though. John recognized it the second he saw Matt's face as he, Caty and Hailey made their way into the kitchen.

He was smiling. Not the half smirk he usually wore, but an all-out grin, as if he'd just heard the best news of his life. John was dying to know what had put that cat-in-cream look on his intense big brother's face, but he sensed there was news to share and didn't want to spoil the moment.

Once they were all settled, Matt folded his hands on the table and glanced around the group that had grown considerably in the past three years. Caty had become a Sawyer, and Ridge had dropped out of the sky to join Marianne and her kids. Seth's quiet presence was a welcome addition to the chaos, keeping Lisa grounded in reality. With Hailey, Drew and Chelsea added to the mix, the old farmhouse was full to bursting.

Ethan would have loved it, John thought fondly. Now, he could think of his father without choking on the guilt he'd carried around for so long. Amanda had helped him put that behind him, and he'd always be grateful to her. But thinking of her made him sad, so he pushed the thought aside to focus on happier things.

As Matt smiled at each of them in turn, he resembled Ethan more than he ever had in his life. John recognized that something important had changed inside his brother, and he suspected Hailey was the reason.

Family, John thought with pride. *This was what it was all about.*

"I've got something to tell all of you," Matt began in his low drawl. After pausing for effect, he went on. "As of five o'clock today, the Sawyer farm is officially out of debt."

Everyone whooped and hollered, and even Tucker joined in, jumping up and down, barking his approval. John knew how the Lab felt.

"That's awesome! But I don't get it," John added in confusion. "We were way short in May. What happened?"

"The price of soybeans doubled in October. Some blight somewhere, so the value of ours went through the roof. Congratulations, Goldilocks. Your crazy experiment put us over the top."

Ridge clapped John on the shoulder. "Nice job."

"I have to admit, I was skeptical," Matt confided.

Caty laughed. "As usual."

"But you were right on the money, John," he continued, ignoring the jab. "Assuming we don't have a drought or flood next year, this farm will actually make money for the first time in ten years. Thanks to you."

His proud smile made John sit up a little straighter, and he nodded his appreciation. Matt didn't often call people out that way—good or bad. That he'd chosen to do it now made it clear just how much John's efforts had meant to the overall health of their family's business.

"That's really cool, Uncle John," Kyle chimed in. "You should plant more soybeans next year."

"Yeah, I should." Rubbing his sore shoulders, he chuckled. "Maybe it'll be easier next time."

"We've got good news, too." Ridge traded grins with Kyle. "Wanna tell them?"

"*Ann Marie*'s almost ready," the boy said excitedly.

Marianne's expression brightened even more than it had with Matt's revelation. "I can't believe it! That's wonderful."

The others piled on their own praise about the

biplane, and then dug into their meals. This was what they'd all been praying and working for. With that huge loan payment off their backs, they could plan for the future instead of putting all their energy into clawing their way out of what had seemed like an inescapable hole. But while he enjoyed the lively banter that moved around the table with the passing of salad and pork roast, he couldn't shake the feeling that something was missing. Someone.

Amanda.

He hadn't heard from her since their blowup two weeks ago. Then again, he'd literally slammed the door on her, and he had no intention of bending on this one. If she went through with the adoption, he couldn't live with the knowledge that she'd given her own child away. Even though he'd come to see that her reasons contained more than a sliver of sense, he couldn't bring himself to accept them.

But she'd refused to marry him, and wouldn't allow him to help her raise the baby otherwise. He loved her more than he'd ever thought possible, and it was killing him to take such a hard line with her when she was in such a vulnerable position. Because of his strong feelings for her, even when they were friends he'd always given in, just to make her happy.

Not this time.

Unaccustomed to handling such thorny problems, he'd prayed a lot about this one. Even with God's help, he kept coming back to the same conclusion.

It had been tough for John to admit, but after a string of sleepless nights, he'd come to terms with the only thing capable of driving a wedge between Amanda and him. On this issue, he simply couldn't compromise.

Children were gifts from God, no matter how they came to be. They weren't something to be cast off because they came along at an inconvenient time. While his marriage proposal might have been clumsy, it had come straight from his foolish heart, and that she'd rejected it definitely stung. He understood the desperation motivating her to consider adoption, and he would always love her because he didn't know how to stop loving her. But emotions wouldn't change the facts, no matter how much he wished things were different.

When he noticed Marianne giving him the worried-mom look, John smiled to ease her concern and started eating. While he did his best to join in the lighthearted conversation, he couldn't shake the terrible feeling that Amanda was driving her life straight over a cliff.

And there was nothing he could do to stop her.

* * *

Amanda couldn't recall how many different positions she'd tried for sleeping tonight. Each one started out fine, then quickly caused just as much pain as the one before. Sitting up was killing her back, so she tried lying down. She attempted it completely stretched out, then rolled to both sides with her legs at as many angles as she could manage with her bulky frame. Finally, around two in the morning, she struggled out of bed to sit up in the armchair. Resting her feet on a step stool, she tipped her head back and was able to doze. For about ten minutes.

The pain returned with a vengeance, so intense it actually took her breath away. She was still a week from her due date, but she started wondering if she might be in labor. No, that wasn't possible, her brain insisted. According to the book she'd all but memorized, nobody delivered her first child early. If anything, she went two weeks overdue and had to be induced.

Suddenly, she was dying of thirst. Wonderful. As if she didn't have enough problems. Sighing to no one, she pushed up from the chair and shuffled into the kitchen to get a glass of water. As she reached into the cupboard, a spasm that made the others feel like simple cramps caught her totally off guard, and she gasped in shock.

She vaguely registered the glass shattering on

the floor, and reached behind her, trying to massage the muscles that were clenched like fists. After what felt like minutes but was more like thirty seconds, things started to relax. And then she felt it.

Liquid trickling down her leg. She couldn't see in the near darkness, but instinct told her that her water had just broken. Soon after, the next wave of pain crashed in, and she dropped to the floor. Balanced on her hands and knees, she carefully avoided the broken glass while she tried to breathe the way she'd learned in Lamaze class. When the contraction passed, she noted the time and gulped in mouthfuls of air.

The next one clobbered her five minutes later.

"Okay, Amanda," she coached herself in a hoarse whisper. "Time to go."

The shuttle to Kenwood didn't run at night, so she had to call an ambulance. Terrified that she'd fall if she stood up, she crawled over to unlock the door for the EMTs. Then she made her way to the bedside table where her phone was charging. She hadn't used it much lately, and when she picked it up, she had to wake it from sleep mode to make the call.

Like some kind of beacon, the home screen photo flashed to life. It was of John with her at the farm, his arms wrapped around her from behind while she snapped the picture. Touching the image, she recalled that beautiful, sunny day, when everything had seemed so perfect. Like a fool, she'd allowed pragmatism to ruin her best chance at happiness.

Why hadn't she deleted this picture? she scolded herself. Memories like this would only make her somber decision more difficult to make. John had offered her everything a woman could want, and in taking such a firm stance on the adoption issue, she'd pretty much thrown it back in his face.

Consumed by regrets and debating what-ifs, she'd unwisely lost track of the minutes ticking by. She was rudely hauled back to reality by a contraction so fierce, it made her drop her cell and double over in agony. The phone hit the table, and from a distance she heard a groggy—and very familiar—voice.

"Amanda?"

By some amazing coincidence, the fall had activated the icon programmed with John's number. Glancing up, she offered a quick but heartfelt prayer of gratitude. "I'm in labor."

"Now?"

"Yes," she ground out between clenched teeth. "Now."

"On my way, Panda. Hang in there."

"John?"

She could hear rustling as he pulled on his jacket. "Yeah?"

"I'm really scared." Hearing the whine in her voice, she pushed aside her usual disgust in favor of comfort. "Please don't hang up."

"No problem." She heard his boots running over gravel, then the welcome sound of his car roaring to life. "Hey, did you hear the Falcons' starting quarterback is healed up and playing Sunday?"

"Really?" She panted. "That's great."

While he rambled along about how much the team needed their star player, she watched the digital seconds ticking away on her phone's timer. Precisely four-and-a-half minutes after he'd answered her call, John came through the door just as another contraction stormed in. He talked her through it, then helped her to her feet.

Rubbing her back in blissful circles, he asked, "Can you handle the stairs?"

"I think so."

She managed a few steps before her legs felt like they'd morphed into rubber. Sweeping her up as if she didn't weigh half a ton, he chuckled, "I think this'll be easier."

Overjoyed to have him here, she rested her head on his shoulder and relinquished control of the situation with a tired sigh. "Okay."

He carted her downstairs and got her belted

into his car. In the haze of headlights, he looked as exhausted as she felt. "You look beat."

"It's the end of harvest season," he replied as he got in beside her and headed out to the highway. "Things always get crazy this time of year."

"All your crops are in? Even the soybeans?"

"Yeah. We paid off the loans, so we're finally back to even."

"That's great, John. Congratulations." Leaning her head back, she breathed through another contraction.

"How far apart are they?"

"Four minutes now. My water broke a while ago."

"Aw, man." He flashed her a grim look. "This is it, then."

She nodded, and he uncharacteristically gripped the wheel firmly in both hands, focusing on the winding road. He maintained a string of idle chatter obviously meant to keep her occupied so she wouldn't freak out about what was coming. In spite of his efforts to distract her, she sensed that he wanted to ask if she was ready for this, if she'd decided what to do with the child who was rapidly making her way into the world.

Sadly, Amanda still had no idea.

As John cradled the tiny bundle in his arms, he grinned over at Amanda. "I think we've got a little extra equipment here." When she gave him a blurry, confused look, he explained. "It's a boy."

"What?" She shook her head. "That's not what the sonogram said."

"They're not foolproof," the nurse reminded her with a giggle. "We get surprises like this occasionally."

So far, John hadn't noticed any indication of whether Amanda was going to keep this child or not. Everything had gone so quickly, she'd barely had time to shed the afghan he'd draped over her shoulders before leaving Ruthy's. Because he firmly believed actions spoke louder than words, he strolled past the medical staff and handed the boy to his mother.

The loving expression that lit her features answered the question that had been dogging him since this huge rift had formed between them, threatening to forever separate him from the woman he loved.

"Oh, just look at him," she breathed, her gaze roving over him from nose to toes. "He's perfect."

"A real cutie, just like his mom."

With a look of wonderment, she ran a trembling fingertip over the baby's cheeks, down to his chin, smiling as his new eyes cracked open and tried to focus on her. "How could I even think of giving him up?"

"That's what I've been waiting to hear." John

leaned in to brush a kiss over her lips, then rested his forehead against hers. "Missed you."

"I missed you, too." Her voice quivering with emotion, she added, "I really needed you tonight, and you didn't let me down. I can never thank you enough for coming."

"Hey, I told you. I'm your guy. One of 'em, anyway," he clarified with a grin. "Any ideas for a name?"

Gazing down at the newborn, she replied, "I've always liked *Aidan*."

"Cool. What do you think of Sawyer?"

"Sawyer Gardner?"

She seemed completely baffled, and he couldn't help laughing. "Not exactly. I love you, Amanda. And this little guy, too," he added, gently tickling the baby's button nose with his finger. "Will you both marry me?"

"Oh, that's so sweet," the nurse cooed, then backpedaled with a blush. "Sorry, but that's about the most romantic thing I've ever seen."

"It sure is." Amanda beamed up at him as if he'd just handed her the keys to a castle. "And totally unlike a Sawyer boy. What's come over you?"

"You," John replied softly. "For me, it's always been you, and it always will be. So whattya say?"

The baby chose that moment to squawk his

opinion, and Amanda gave a tired laugh. Kissing her son's forehead, she met John's hopeful gaze with misty eyes.

"We say yes."

Epilogue

❧

Thanksgiving morning, Amanda was in the Sawyers' kitchen giving Aidan his midmorning bottle when she noticed a strange buzzing sound overhead. It kept getting louder, as if a giant wasp was closing in on the farm.

"No way!" Kyle yelled, racing in from the living room where he and Emily had been watching the parade on TV. She was close on his heels, and Marianne was only a couple of steps behind them.

As the screen door slammed behind them, through the window Amanda saw a maroon-and-white biplane zooming along, about ten feet off the ground. When she thought for sure it would crash into the tall equipment barn, the plane climbed into the sky and did an impossible loop.

John came out of the pantry with two huge platters. Setting them on the counter, he chuckled. "That's Ridge for you. Always full of surprises."

"He didn't tell anyone he was flying the plane home today?" she asked, easing the bottle back when she noticed Aidan was fast asleep.

"Nope, not even Kyle. Marianne used to hate that, but I guess she doesn't mind it so much anymore."

"Ridge kind of grows on people," Caty agreed as she got Hailey some animal crackers from the jar on the counter.

The mention of his best friend's charm made Matt snort good-naturedly. "Yeah, like fungus. No matter how hard you try, you can't get rid of him."

John and Seth had their heads together over some large papers spread out over the table, and Lisa leaned in to see what they were doing. "This looks good. Three bedrooms upstairs, with a bathroom. The lower level will be nice, wide-open living space."

"Listen to Mrs. HGTV over there," John teased Seth. "How do you live with that?"

"Pretty easy."

Although he spoke to John, Seth's smile was directed at his wife, who rewarded him with a peck on the cheek on her way to the fridge. It had taken a while, but Amanda was finally accustomed to the chaotic energy that filled every inch of the Sawyer farm. The house and barns, the fields surrounding them, even the sky, she thought as Ridge's beloved *Ann Marie* buzzed overhead.

It was crazy, but happy. And she thanked God for making her part of it.

"This looks bigger than what you have now," Amanda commented while she assessed the blueprints. "Are you sure this will all fit?"

John traded a grin with his brother-in-law. "Sure, we're sure. We're expanding it." Pointing to one side, he explained, "We'll blow out this wall and double the size of the house on both levels. That'll give us a huge great room and a nice, big office for you. With the way CPR is growing, you're gonna need it."

"Are those French doors on my office?"

"Yes, ma'am. You'll have a view of the pond while you're working."

He was so excited, she hated to rain on his insane parade. But someone had to be practical, and it appeared that she was elected. "This kind of project is way beyond what you and Seth can do yourselves, so we're going to need an actual construction crew. How are we paying for all this?"

Sitting next to her, John leaned in for a quick kiss. "Dad left me some money, and I still have it. I never felt right about spending it before, but I think he'd be happy if I used it to spruce up the carriage house."

Not even a hint of sorrow dimmed the enthusiasm shining in his eyes, and she was thrilled to see it. "Sounds good to me."

"Cool." When he noticed the list she'd been making, he gently bumped shoulders with her. "How many wedding guests are we talking about?"

"Sixty. Since it's December tenth, Danielle Benton said she can make our cake before she gets too busy with her Christmas orders. I wanted to pay for it, but she wants it to be her wedding gift to us."

"That's fantastic. I had a blast sampling her latest batch of inventions."

Amanda slanted him a suspicious look, and he held up his hands innocently. "Never dated her. Honest."

"One of the few," she teased. "You should probably write them all down so I know who to watch out for after we're married."

"You're still sure you want to do it so soon?"

"Definitely." It had been her idea not to wait, and she hadn't changed her mind. If anything, she was more eager now that she'd seen the designs for their house.

While she and John debated chocolate, vanilla or marble cake, the Collinses came trooping inside, with a panting Tucker close behind.

"Crazy Lab." Holding Emily in his arms, Ridge reached down to ruffle the dog's floppy ears. "He chased me all the way in from the woodlot. I think he's as excited about seeing *Ann Marie* in the air as we are."

"She's beautiful, Daddy," Emily announced. "The colors I picked look very pretty up in the sky."

"When I'm grown-up, you can teach me to fly her," Kyle said confidently. "And then I'll teach Drew and Aidan when they're old enough."

"More pilots in the family," Marianne groaned, her fond smile easing the complaint. "Just what we need."

But Amanda had latched on to Kyle's offer. "You're going to teach Aidan?"

"Sure." He shrugged as if it was no big deal. "He's my cousin just like Hailey, so I'll watch out for him."

"Me, too," Emily promised eagerly. "We'll take care of all the younger kids. That's what families do."

That's what families do.

Sweet and simple, Amanda saw that sentiment reflected in the nods and smiles that rippled through the diverse group clustered around the table. More than a piece of furniture, she recalled John telling her, it had been in that spot since the 1850s. Tradition and history—that's what the Sawyers had, what had always been missing from her own life.

Until now.

Because in asking her to be his wife, John had made both her and Aidan part of this amazing family. Even with all the baubles and fancy jewelry she'd once owned, no one had ever offered her something so precious.

Her soon-to-be-husband nudged her elbow. "Earth to Amanda."

"Sorry." She covered her embarrassment with a smile. "What?"

"What do you think of our ideas?" he asked, nodding at the plans.

Shifting Aidan so he was cuddled between them, she leaned against John with a contented sigh. "I think it's the perfect place for a family."

"Me, too," he answered, standing as a strange car pulled up outside.

When he held an arm out for her, she shook her head. "Aidan just fell asleep. I'm not moving for a couple of hours."

"I think he'll want to be awake for this."

She couldn't begin to guess what John meant, but she stood and followed him onto the porch. When the driver stepped out of the car, she couldn't believe what she was seeing. "Dad?"

"Just to be clear," he began, holding his hands in front of him like a shield. "This was your mother's idea."

"Oh, stop it, Harry," a tiny blond woman scolded

as she hurried over to embrace Amanda. "Don't pay him any attention at all, sweetheart. He wanted to see you as much as I did. He's just too mule-headed to admit it," she added with a chiding glare over her shoulder.

"So that's where Amanda gets it from," John commented lightly, blowing the tension away with a confident grin. After a hug for her mom, he offered a hand to her standoffish father. "I'm glad you two could make it. We've got an awful lot of food in there."

Amanda was a quick study, and she turned to her meddling fiancé with an accusing look. "You called my parents?"

The fool didn't even blink. "This is Aidan's first Thanksgiving. I figured his grandparents should be here. Don't you?"

"Well, yes, but—"

"Stop talking and hand over that handsome boy," Mom interrupted, taking him from Amanda's arms. He blinked up at her, then gave her a baby smirk. Closing her eyes, she cuddled him close. "It's so nice to meet you, Aidan."

Dad fished an envelope from his inner jacket pocket and handed it to John. "Just a little something for the nursery. Babies are expensive."

His comments were gruff, but as he watched Aidan, there was a softening around his eyes. After a few moments, the frown he normally wore mellowed into something dangerously like a smile.

"Thank you so much." When Amanda hugged him, he stiffened at first but quickly relaxed.

"You're welcome, punkin." As he gazed down at her, regret showed in his dark eyes. "I only wish I'd done it sooner."

Harry Gardner was a very proud man, and she knew it took a lot of courage for him to admit he'd been wrong to turn away from her. Proud tears welled in her eyes, and she forgave him on the spot.

"Does this mean you've reconsidered about walking me down the aisle?"

After a quick grimace, he nodded. "I should never have said no in the first place."

"Water under the bridge."

All hatchets buried, they walked through the door and everyone greeted her parents. The huge table was crowded with food, and for the first time Amanda saw the two extra places that had been set. She'd been so focused on Aidan, she hadn't noticed them before, and she marveled at the Sawyers' ability to keep a secret.

Once they were all seated, Matt, the one-time black sheep, folded his hands in front of him on the table and looked around with a warm smile. "Happy Thanksgiving, everyone."

"Happy Thanksgiving," they all replied, smiling at each other.

"We've been through a lot the past few years." Grasping Caty's hand, he went on, "And even though we had a rocky start, I want to say how proud I am to be the head of this family. Most days," he added, sending a mock glare down the table at John.

"One word, big brother," he shot back with a grin. "Soybeans."

"He's got you there," Lisa teased, blowing Matt an air kiss while the others laughed.

It was a warm, cozy moment, perfectly suited to a day devoted to showing gratitude for the blessings in your life. Shifting a fussy Drew to her other shoulder, Marianne lifted her water glass. "To family."

Those simple words wrapped around Amanda's heart, and she cuddled Aidan a little closer. Smiling at each other, she and John clinked glasses and then raised them up toward the center of the table.

"To family."

* * * * *

If you enjoyed this story by Mia Ross,
be sure to check out the other books
this month from Love Inspired!

Dear Reader,

I hope you enjoyed reading Amanda and John's story as much as I did writing it. Sometimes it's fun to think about what would happen if you met up with a long-lost friend again. Sometimes it's not.

Some people change to the point where we don't recognize them anymore, as Amanda had. Or they're like John, who's remained constant over the years. We often discover they've settled somewhere in the middle, so we still recognize the friend we remember but can appreciate the changes we see. Whatever the case, keeping an open mind is the best way to resurrect an old relationship. It may not be easy, but it just might be worth the effort.

If you'd like to stop by for a visit, you'll find me online at www.miaross.com, and on Facebook and Twitter. While you're there, send me a message in your favorite format. I'd love to hear from you!

Mia Ross

Questions for Discussion

1. When Amanda arrives at the farm, her appearance has changed so much that John doesn't recognize her. Have you ever come across someone you knew a long time ago who's changed to that degree? Did you consider those changes good or bad?

2. Sometimes, when people move away, in trying to start fresh they neglect where they came from. Are you like that, or do you have fond memories of the past?

3. John hasn't changed much since high school, which Amanda thinks is a good thing. What do you think?

4. The old saying "Bloom where you're planted" really applies to John. Do you believe that, or should people strive for something more?

5. When Amanda's parents discover her situation, they refuse to help her. John suggests they might change their minds someday, but Amanda's not so sure. When they show up for Thanksgiving, she's stunned by their turnaround. Have you ever been surprised in a similar way?

6. While Amanda takes several crushing blows to her pride, she never loses the spirit John always admired. Have you been confronted with the same kinds of challenges? How did you handle them?

7. John feels responsible for his father's death and has been struggling to forgive himself. With Amanda's help, he's finally able to think of Ethan in a positive way. Have you ever felt you had to forgive yourself for something? How did you get to the point where you could move on?

8. Amanda has lost her connection to the faith she was raised with. John thinks that's why she has so much trouble accepting setbacks in her life. Do you know people who've drifted away from God and been grateful to find their way back again?

9. When Amanda sees the window in the church, she spots a shadow in the design John never noticed before. Have you ever seen a work of art in which you notice certain things while someone else sees something else entirely? Do you think artists intend that, or do we see what we're looking for?

10. Ruthy knows Amanda's situation even before she's told. Are you or is someone you know intuitive that way? If so, how does that intuition affect the lives of others?

11. At the end of the story, John lays out his plans for enlarging his house to make room for a bigger family. When Amanda asks where the money is coming from, he tells her he now feels comfortable spending some of the money his father left him. Have you ever been in a situation where you needed to settle something in the past before tackling something in the future? If so, how did it work out?

LARGER-PRINT BOOKS!

GET 2 FREE
LARGER-PRINT NOVELS
PLUS 2 FREE
MYSTERY GIFTS

Love Inspired®

Larger-print novels are now available...

ReaderService.com

Manage your account online!

- Review your order history
- Manage your payments
- Update your address

*We've designed
the Harlequin® Reader Service
website just for you.*

Enjoy all the features!

- Reader excerpts from any series
- Respond to mailings and
  special monthly offers
- Discover new series available to you
- Browse the Bonus Bucks catalog
- Share your feedback

Visit us at:
ReaderService.com